Elizabeth Yates Richmond

Poems of the Western Land

Elizabeth Yates Richmond

Poems of the Western Land

ISBN/EAN: 9783743348943

Manufactured in Europe, USA, Canada, Australia, Japa

Cover: Foto ©Andreas Hilbeck / pixelio.de

Manufactured and distributed by brebook publishing software (www.brebook.com)

Elizabeth Yates Richmond

Poems of the Western Land

POEMS

OF THE

ESTERN LAND.

BY

ELIZABETH YATES RICHMOND.

"Come to me with your triumphs and your woes,
    Ye forms, to life by glorious poets brought—
I sit alone with flowers and vernal boughs
    In the deep shadow of a voiceless thought ;
'Midst the glad music of the spring alone,
And sorrowful for visions that are gone !
                    —*Mrs. Hemans.*"

HOPEKAH,

THE WINNEBAGO PRINCESS.

PREFACE.

That our own beautiful state might produce, at
the touch of the magician's wand, romances and heroic
tales, weird and uncanny as any told by Scandinavian
scald, or Highland minstrel, who can doubt?

The wild tribes we have swept out before us,
whose snow-shoes have long since disappeared beyond
the mountains, have left us to gather their chronicles
and legends as best we may, from the archives of the
forest, or the sarcophagus by the torrent.

And though their folios have been entrusted to the
limestone boulders, and their manuscripts to the
autumn leaves that the December hurricanes have
swept into the great lakes, still we stumble upon frag-
ments now and then that marshal before us Chief and
Sachem in their bravery, with all the love and hate
of those elder days.

Such is the story of the Winnebago Princess,
whose home stood upon the shores of the beautiful
lake, more than one hundred years ago, (probably on

what is now called "The Island," on which stands part of the city of Neenah), in northern Wisconsin.

Here stands yet, in the unscathed vigor of centuries, the ancient "Council Tree," "planted by the rivers of waters," whose leaf has not withered, though generation after generation have passed from under it.

Across the lake, on the eastern shore, is the line of cliffs, standing like walls of olden castles, and formerly used as hiding-places for the warriors.

Beyond, on the western shore, is the historical "Hill of the Dead," where French, Sacs and Foxes fell in deadly combat, through which our civilized vandals have recently laid the track for one of their railroads.

The whole of the picturesque lake-shore is full of wild romance and weird story, that only awaits the pen of a Walter Scott to bring it out.

On these broad shores dwelt the Winnebago Queen, Ho-po-ho-e-kau, or Hopekah, (Glory of the Morning.) Here, according to Carver and Gale, she was born, and here she died. Here she entertained the traders who wandered to those far-away shores:

led her councils, and advised her warriors, then numerous and strong. Here she married the French Captain, De Kaury, who was afterwards shot at the siege of Quebec, when Gen. Wolfe fell before the "Heights of Abraham."

Of her grave and last res'ing-place the winds tell us not. We only know that her sons, and sons' sons, or several generations succeeded her in the chieftain-ship; but her people, and the gnarled old cedars that sheltered them,—where are they ?

E. Y. R.

RIVERSIDE COTTAGE, Appleton, Wis., Sept. 7, 1878.

POEMS

—OF THE—

WESTERN LAND.

HOPEKAH,

THE WINNEBAGO PRINCESS.

Where the blue-waved Winnebago   .
Sat among her fringe of forests,
Chorusing adown the ages
    Anthems of that elder time—
While upon her purple border,
Purple with the mists of autumn,
Stood the cedars in their glory,
    Stood the hemlock and the pine;
And the oaks, with tarnished helmets,
And the elms, with cloaks of gold,
Bowing low like reverent courtiers
    To the wild lake as it rolled,—

Rolled in turbulence, or silence,
  With its voices manifold.

There the red sun of September,
Climbing wearily the ramparts
Of the heavens, that sultry evening,
  Like a heated troubadour
Breathless from the fight and foray,
With his scarlet mantle flying
  To the windward, as he tore
O'er the forests and the prairies,
O'er the cliff and o'er the marshes,
  To old Winnebago's shore;
There he dipped his molten sandals,
Tossed his red cloak on the waters,
Dashed with spray his heated forehead—
Till the forest laughed and reveled
  At the garish robes they wore
At the burnished scarfs of scarlet
  Flung o'er larch and sycamore.

And the smoky heavens above him
Open swung their western portal—
Swung upon their golden hinges
  Widely their unbolted gate;
And through battlements of cloudland—
Through those dim, mysterious regions,
  Where the patient planets wait,

Passed the hot and breathless racer,
Up the war-trail of the Sachems;
    And the woods, disconsolate,
Saw their fading glories perish,
Hung their mournful heads in silence,
    Erst with glory all elate.

In her wigwam by the lakeshore
Watched the Indian maid Hopekah—
Watched the light canoes, that flitting
    Laden past her lodge of bark,
Many a tired and weary warrior,
With his skins of deer and panther,
    Homeward bore, before the dark.
Till upon the sand-beach bounding,
Stood a brown and stalwart chieftain,
    Freighted with the forest spoils;
Heavy round his neck the wampum,
Heavy hung his brow with feathers
    Plucked from many a distant isle;
And his step was bold and fearless
As the monarch of the desert,
While he sought his birchen wigwam
    Where the maiden sat the while—
Sat and welcomed from his hunting
    Thus her sire, with song and smile,—

"The eagle has fled to her eyrie beyond,
    And the loon to her bed 'mong the reeds;

And the young fawns moan in the forest alone
  Where their panting mother bleeds.

And the fledgelings call from their home in the sedge
  By the side of the reedy lake,
For the blue-winged heron that comes not back
  Through the tangled brush and brake.

And the wild dove so softly coos to her young,
  Beyond in the forest afar;
Come again to thy lodge, my warrior sire,
  By the light of the shooting star.

All day I have watched where the torch of the braves
  The slumbering forests fired,
Till my brow grew hot 'neath its band of beads,
  And my cheek grew flushed and tired.

I have beaded thy pouch, I have tinted thy bow:
  Thy mat 'neath the vines is unrolled;
So welcome thee back to thy lodge by the lake,
  My warrior Sachem bold."

    O'er the Sachem's swarthy visage
    Crept awhile the softening shadows,
    And the mouth, so stern and rigid,
    Grew as tender as a woman's
        When a babe looks in her face;
    And upon the maiden's shoulder—

Brown, but round and classic-moulded—
Smiling flung the strings of wampum,
    And the trophies of the chase;
Feathers dipped in gold and carmine:
Wing of teal and plume of heron;
Purpling clusters of the autumn,
    From the vines that interlace
All the hunter's tangled pathway
    Through the fern and sassafras.

Precious was this child unto him:
Daughter of his dead Nehotah,
Whose lone grave among the grasses
    Many an autumn's moon had kissed;
Many a winter's snow had fallen,
Many a spring-time's flowers had blossomed
    Since beyond him, through the mist,
On a summer cloud she vanished,—
Vanished like an uncaged oriole
    Up the paths of amethyst.

Vanished through the twilight shadow—
Through the interminable footpaths
    Eye nor ken have ever guessed,
Where the misty spirit-lodges
    Stud the far fields of the West;
Leaving among the mats of rushes,

Deft and curiously enwoven,
    One small fledgeling in her nest.

Strange that this dark-visaged chieftain,
With his panther-skin about him,
And his brow with eagle's feathers
    And with painted plumes bedight,
Turned so oft to gaze unnoticed
On the little waif that slumbered
Softly in its birch-bark cradle,
    Through the day and through the night;
Yet unto the lake-shore Sachem
    That imperious, dusky wight,
Centered all the blood of warriors
Through the rushing ages mingling;
    Thus, by fate's strange oversight,
Mingling in this tiny maiden,
Frail and fair, and slightly fashioned—
Heir of stalwart forest princes,
Who, though fit for fight nor foray,
For the war-path or the battle,
Still might wear her father's wampum
    Proudly as a belted knight.

So she slept, and grew and flourished,
And the summers and the winters
    Passed uncounted o'er her head;
And the ancient squaw that watched her

"Glory of the Morning" called her:
  Decked her well with fringe and bead—
Twined her raven tress with vine-wreaths,
  Or with bitter sweet instead,
Till its orange berries circled,
Peerless as the the pearls of countess,
  Her brown brow unbonneted.

Never fear nor danger awed her,
For the smothered blood of heroes
  Sex, nor age, nor form can stay;
Wandered she the pathless forests,
Climbed unhelped the rugged cliff-tops,
  All in her wild disarray;
Learned to shoot her father's arrows;
Scaled the tall perch of the eagle,
Cooing softly to the eaglets,
Pressing them upon her bosom—
  Daring not to bear away
From the lonely absent mother
  Foraging for fish or prey,
One soft downy half-fledged nestling,
Lest the homeward bird returning
  Flutter with a strange dismay.

Deft was she, and fairy-fingered;
  And through stormy wintry moons,
When the tempest howled, and reveled,

Chanting past some weirdish rune,
By the wigwam firelight sat she.
With her beads, and painted grasses,
Broidering cunningly her vestments, ·
 Kirtles gay, and dainty shoon,
Jackets for the chief, her father,
 Quaintly as from ancient loom;
All the while she sat and broidered,
Chorusing the old lake's dirges
 With some half-forgotten tune.

One bright morn the hunters' echoes,
Long, and loud, and far resounding,
 Swept across the breezy lake;
And as start the wild Bedouins
From their unsuspected coverts,
 Yak or ghau to overtake;
So that elfish horde of hunters,
Supple-limbed, and strong and stalwart,
 All their painted plumage shake,
Crowd the arrows in their pouches,
Whet their knives upon the flint-stones—
 And the sleeping forests wake,
Till the snow-enshrouded cedars
 To their topmost branches quake.

Springing from his bed of rushes
Bounded forth the lake-shore Sachem,

And his heavy wolf-skin jacket
   O'er his massive shoulders flung:
And his elfish locks of midnight,
Blacker than the the condor's plumage,
   Round his dusky forehead clung;
And his broidered pouch of arrows
   O'er his stately neck he slung,
While his polished hatchet, glistening,
   Down upon the hearth-stone rung.

All the lights and shadows flickered
For a moment, quick and transient,
On the brow of fair Hopekah,
   As the gorgeous cavalcade
Flitted past her father's door-way,
O'er the icy lake that morning
   In their brilliant masquerade;
And with eyes all dark and glowing,
   Gazing at the weird brigade,
Thus the winsome forest beauty,
   Pleading to her father, said,—

"Let me go, let me go! where the forests a-shiver
Their icicles shake o'er the desolate river;
Where the panther screams down from his nest 'mong
   the fir,
And the hemlocks their boughs to the wintry winds
   stir.

Let me go where the black bear hath chosen to
    slumber,
Among the cavernous rocks of the grey cliff-tops
    yonder;
Where the antelope bounds and the wa-wa is calling;
And the long-bearded moss from the cedars is falling.

Let me clamber the rocks! let me carry thy quiver!
And my snow-shoes shall bound o'er the broad frozen
    river;
And my arrow shall speed through the grim woods
    unerring,
And my step o'er the crags shall climb free and un-
    fearing."

The Sachem, with his belt unbuckled,
Listened proudly to his daughter;
Watched her firm heroic features,
    Fired with daring of her race.
All the courage of her fathers,
Whom the mosses long had covered,
    Slept unquestioned in that face;
While her woman's nature lent her
    All the spells of softer grace.

"Hie thee, then, my daughter," quoth he;
"Wrap thy warm blue-bordered blanket
Closely round thy slender shoulders;

And about thy raven hair
Bind thy scarf of scarlet closely:
Fasten well thy beaded buskins;
And my crest of heron's feathers
    Thou upon thy brow shalt wear.
Haste, my dauntless mountaineer,
For already gleam the hatchets
    In the forest paths afar."

All that day was fair and golden
On the shores of Winnebago;
And the winds just stopped to whisper
    Where, aloof from shot and targe,
Sleeping in the lonely cloisters
    Of the lake-shore's utmost verge,
Lay the grey wolf and the panther,
    In some grim embattled gorge;
While along the winding war-trails
Stealthy ranks of weird banditti
    From the snow-wreathed woods emerge;
And the torches lit the hill-tops;
And the hunter's broad knives glistened
    Like new sword-blades from the forge.

Perched upon the walls of limestone *
By some vanished ocean left us,—

* The Clifton Heights on the east shore of Lake Winnebago, one of the most romantic nooks in Wisconsin.

Some broad sea, that fast receding,
    Left its solid ramparts yet,
Though the waves that thundered round it
By the rushing centuries silenced,
    Long have ceased to roar and fret—
There upon those cliff-tops circling,
Round their hunter's fire assembling
    Chief and brave their ruth forget;
And the hunting-song floats downward
    O'er that rocky parapet,—

"Spirit of the lordly hunters
    Sleeping on through shine and storm,
Come and point our painted arrows,
    Bend our bow, and nerve our arm;
Show us where the panther wrestles,
Show us where the white swan nestles,
    Where the blue-winged wild-ducks swarm.

Spirit of the ancient hunters,
    Point to us the sleeping bear;
Lay your silent finger on him
As he slumbers in his cavern—
    In his cavern grim and drear;
Show us where the the tall elk passes
O'er the brake and withered grasses;
    Where the conies disappear.

Wake again, O buried Sachems!
Wait we till your steeds again
Down the pathway of the Westland
　　Cleave the startled clouds in twain;
And unto your olden places,
With the war-paint on your faces,
　　Lead with daring strides our van."

So, adown the cliffs resounding,
Swelled the song, and flared the pine-boughs,
Waking in the speechless forests
　　Long redoubled semibreves;
Sending tremorous notes of terror
Through the undiscovered chancels
　　Of those ghostly spirit-caves,
Till they rocked from base to center,
　　And their rocky architraves
Quaked in mingled fear and wonder
　　At the chorus of the braves.

Suddenly,'a deer espying,
Bounding past them from its covert,
With its lordly horns uplifted
　　In a frightened escapade,
Down the cliff-sides dashed the cohorts—
Over limestone ledge and bastion,
　　Mossy niche and colonnade,
Swinging from the hanging tree-trunks

Which their onward course delayed—
Down upon the rushing courser,
Tangled by his branching antlers
  In the hidden ambuscade.

All that day in short December,—
With the transient sun out-riding
  Like a heated cavalier,—
Tore they over hill and valley,
Through the fen and through the fastness;
  Clambering over crag and scar,
Till the day wore to its closing,
And the western archways opening,
  Crimson curtains seemed to wear.

Never heard old Winnebago
O'er her ice-environed waters
  Such a noisy roundelay;
Never held upon her bosom,
Sheathed and mailed in solid crystal,
  Such a gallant holiday;
Never counted 'mong her courtiers
  Such a marvelous array,
As when brave, and chief, and warrior,
Round their hunting feast-fire gathering,
  Brought their trophies of the fray.

All the board with royal rations,
Fit for Sheik or Sultan, laden,

And with dishes multiform,
Spread in wild barbaric bounty,
    Gartered Knight nor Khan need scorn;
And athwart the shadows creeping,
Scaring weendigoes and demons,
    Clearly blew the hunting-horn;

That loud blast that far resounding
    O'er the hill-side and the slope,
Gathered many a recreant hunter
Straying 'mong the brush and tangles,
And with heavy booty laden
    Peering from the cliffs a-top.

With deliberate step, and stately,
Strolled the Sachem of the Lakeside,
And his daughter, fair Hopekah,
    Gazing on the motley troop;
He, with hides and antlers laden;
She, with birds of gaudy plumage—
While among her dark hair twisted,
    Golden berries twine and group,
And about her cheek of carmine
    In their tangled clusters droop.

By their side a stranger hunter,
With his gun and flask of powder—
Who, in search of hides and peltries,

By some fortunate mischance,
Straying from his mates that morning,
O'er the forest's broad expanse,—
Came upon the dark-eyed huntress,
Watching in her vigilance
O'er a den of captured foxes,
Peeping from their cells of limestone,
With their sharp eyes all askance.

Filled his face with admiration
As this daughter of the Sachems,
This untrammeled scion of princes,
Met his dark eye with her own;
In her broidered shoon and kirtle,
And her crest of golden berries
Twisted like an elfish crown
Round her heavy braids all glossy,
Round her tresses backward thrown,
Somewhat tangled by the breezes
That across the lake had blown.

Never valiant crusader,
Riveted to Moorish turret
By some witch in maiden's guise,
Paused amid his clanking armor,
Taken by such sweet surprise
As that stranger knight that morning,

Speaking with a stranger accent—
Waiting only strange replies
From this naiad of the westland,
Who her rustic court was holding
   On the mossy precipice.

Bold and fearless looked this stranger,
With an air that well betokened
   Courtly grace and noble guild;
Dressed in coat of shaggy bear-skin
Pillaged from the coastland mountains,
While the sash and stars he carried
   Told of trophies in the field.

Flinging from him sash and sabre,
Darted down the agile hunter,
   Down the rocks, precipitate;
While upon her rugged outpost,
   Cheeks aflush and eyes dilate,
Sat the still, astonished huntress;
Watched his disappearing footsteps
Down the dank and slippery passage,
   Down the pathway steep and straight.

Once or twice his flint-lock echoed
O'er those pre-historic ramparts;
   Then, with forehead all be-dew,
With a gracious smile, and knightly,

Down his bushy freight of foxes
  At the maiden's feet he threw;
Just as backward from their marches
  Filed the Sachem's retinue.

As around life's camp-fires lonely,
Or in unaccustomed places
  'Mid the desert solitude,
Many a brave meets brave unquestioned;
Many a hand in loyal homage—
  Spanning space and latitude,
Gives the generous clasp of brother,
  Scorns the barrier tint of blood,—
So those two wide-severed chieftains,
From the sunrise and the sunset,
Looked into each other's faces
  With a quick solicitude;
Read the untranslated message
  Each unto the other showed;
And among those rocky ramparts
And interminable forests,
  Hid forever ruth and feud.

'Mong that horde of hungry hunters
Gleamed the stranger's stars that evening;
Told he of his hunts and marches,
Of the country of his people
  O'er the mighty land-locked seas;

How their great ships plowed the waters,
How their cities strewed the coastland,
    Watched by frowning batteries;
Of their great French Father's message
Sent them from his distant castles;
Of the ships that, overladen,
    Sped to them upon the breeze,
Freighted well with guns and blankets,
Scarlet cloth and polished hatchets,
    Piled on stately argosies.*

Listened they with eyes all eager
To the pale-faced captain's story,
Told them in their native jargon
    By a sage who conn'd their speech;
Listened as the rock-bound seaman
    Listens o'er the surge-swept beach
To the great world's distant murmurs,—
    Pausing ever to beseech
Of the winds that whistle by him
Through th' untraversable pathways
    Voice, or message back to fetch.

From his belt the lake-shore Sachem
Silent drew his red-stone peace-pipe;

---

* The vessels of John Jacob Astor and others sent by the French government.

Silent lit it in the embers,
　　Blew a whiff toward the West,
Watched it vanish into darkness,—
　　Then the calumet relighting,
　　　　Turned and passed it to his guest:
And while upward curled the vapor
　　　　Thus his confidence expressed,—

"Brother from the distant sunrise,
From beyond the great sea-water,
Stay thou here among our lodges:
　　　　Spread thy mat beside our door,
'Mong the coves of flags and rushes
　　　　Leave thy bark and painted oar.
Till aloud the Great far Spirit
Calls to thee across the mountains,—
Calls thee back beyond the ledges
　　　　Where the thundering cataracts roar; *
Where thy fathers' graves lie scattered
　　　　'Neath the oak and sycamore."

Thus it was that by the camp-fires
Of the Winnebago warriors
Sat the captain, bold De Kaury,
　　　　Through the wild and wintry moons;
Sat beneath the antlered doorway,

* Niagara.

Sat beneath the painted curtains,
  Through those frosty afternoons,—
Listening while the whirlwind whistled
Through the unhabitable forests,
  Telling o'er his doleful runes.

Loud and noisy swept the snow-blast:
Fierce and cold the bleak northwester,
Just uncaged from icy caverns
  O'er the compassless expanse
Of the great seas, stretching northward—
Whose wild wave had rolled in silence
Since the hemisphere was cradled,
With no prow or keel to measure
  Its supreme circumference.

Through the Sachem's lonely causeway
Snorted loud the great frost-dragon,
With his huge paws tossing upward
  Towering pyramids of snow;
Obelisks that glared and glistened
In that deathly wintry midnight
Like a crew of sheeted specters,
  Wading those dark cedars through;
And beneath his white embankments
Lay and slumbered many a wigwam,
  In the solitude below,—
Slumbered like the storied cities

'Neath the sand-drifts of the cycles,
Sepulchered so long ago.

But upon her mat of rushes,
In her warm blue-bordered blanket,
Broidering still her beaded pouches,
Sat she there—the fair Hopekah,
Through those dismal wintry days,
Sat upon her couch of marsh-grass,
While the pine-boughs flashed and flickered;
And beside her sat the stranger
With his rapt admiring gaze,—
Wondering if so fair Sultana
Sat on velvet mat of princes,
'Neath their gilded canopies.

Patiently, from pictured pages
Taught he to the lake-side maiden
All his country's lore and language;
Taught her of his faith and creed,
Of the prowess of his people,
Of their palaces of splendor,
Of their forts, that o'er the waters
Opened loud their cannonade.

She, the while, with wondering glances,
And with keen perception soaring
To the boundary of his thought,—

From his word, his glance, his gesture,
    Quick his inspiration caught.
Thus, ere well she conned the chapters
From those quaint, mysterious pages,
To her passionate soul receptive
    Love's great lesson he had taught;
And his piercing eye grew softer,
    With a tenderer impulse fraught,
And her cheeks, like autumn russets,
Glowed with deeper tints of carmine
    Than the blazing pine-boughs wrought.

Strange, that this self-banished captain,
Wandering westward for adventure
    From his home across the gulf—
Seeking in the tangled war-paths
Of the "Great French Father's" borders
    Avenues for trade or pelf,
Thus should capture in her fortress
    Unbesieged, this forest elf,
On whose mat both brave and sachem
Vainly tossed their plumes and wampum;
Vainly tuned their pipes of reed-stems,
Pouring out lost adorations
    To the wayward Indian sylph.

Strange, and unexplained the riddle—
Yet the old chief from his corner,

From beneath his shaggy eye-brows
    Read the puzzle through and through;
Smiling quaintly as he read it,
    Caring not to disallow
To this petted waif of chieftains,
    Love's impulsive overflow.
So the twain conned on their lessons,
    Through the shine and through the snow;
And the January tempests
    Through the birchen roof that blew,
Heard amid their fitful pauses
    Many a whispered interview.

Thus it was that when the black-wing,
Gathering all her noisy cohorts,
    Chattered in the coves beyond,
Of the great bergs drifting northward
To the land of snow and shadow,
Where the eider-duck was sailing
    In the solitude profound—

That the two clasped hands together,
Standing on the mat of wolf-skin
    'Neath the rustic wigwam porch,
While beneath them roared the waters,
Breaking up their icy barriers;
And above them, flared the flambeau
    And the blazing tamarack torch—

Glinting on the ranks of warriors
In their scarlet blankets mantled,
  Waiting 'neath the cedar's arch.

All night long the ancient Father *
Far and patiently had ridden,
  With his dusky-visaged guide,
Thus to clasp their hands together
In his church's olden fashion,
  As they stood there side by side,—
She, the Great far Spirit's daughter,
He, at Christian altars bending;
Thus in vows of love united,
  By his blessing ratified.

And the old lake roared compliance—
Woke her slumbering orchestra:
  Thundered forth a marriage hymn;
While upon her shores more softly,
From beneath their braided tresses
  Broke the Indian maids' refrain,—

"Wilt thou go, wilt thou go,
  From the Sachem's door?

* Father Claude Allouez, who established missions at
Green Bay and other points along the Fox river.

Wilt thou tie thy skiff
'Mong the sedge no more?

Wilt thou sit on the mat
Of this pale-faced brave,
Where the moons roll on
By a stranger wave?

Wilt thou roam no more
Where the eaglets sleep?
Where the painted doves
Through the green woods sweep?

Where the sun-fish leaps
To the pebbly strand,
And the white swan feeds
From thy dainty hand?

In the long dark moons
Thy lonely sire
Will wait for thee
By the wigwam fire.

And who shall sing him
The olden song
As lonely he wanders
The cliffs among?"

This the song whose mournful cadence
Rolled along the sandy beaches—
Murmured through the stricken forests,
　　Through the yet unblossoming wood;
While in solemn diapasons
　　Came the sad lake's interlude,
Waking with its incantations
　　All that solemn solitude.

How the feast was spread that evening
'Neath th' entanglement of grape-vines,
Ask the grim ancestral oak trees—
　　Nursed and cradled by the wave,
Ask the moss-enshrouded beeches,
That unto the Sachem's daughter
　　Parting benedictions gave,—
Those lone watchmen of the forest,
Sworn through long centennial ages
　　Storm and whirlwind to outbrave.

Down their war-trails, through the forest,
In their buskins came the chieftains;
Came the chieftains on their mustangs,
　　Bidden to the marriage feast;
Each with belt, and bow, and wampum,
And with crest of painted plumage,
　　For the regal banquet dressed.

Came the lordly Yellow Thunder,
From his lodge among the sumachs;
Came the Grey Wolf from his prowling
    Down along the tamarack slope;
Came with snowy tufts of feathers
O'er his bleaching scalp-locks falling,
Old White Eagle, from his perches,
    Where he watched the antelope;
While the Angry Bear stole downward
    From his den the cliffs a-top,
And with beetling brows of midnight
    Glared in wonder on the group.

'Mong his sun-browned guests assembled
Walked with courtly grace the bridgroom—
Shook their tawny hands with pleasure,
    Smoked with them the calumet;
Scattered friendly gifts among them—
Knives, and beads, and painted trinkets—
Thus in loyal clanship bound them.
And with fealty undissembled,
    Hasting to reciprocate,
'Mong his curling locks they twisted
Spotted plumes of heron's feathers;
Hung around his neck the wampum,
Led him to the mat of rushes
    Where the chiefs and sachems sate;
Bade him sit in council with them,

Lead their talks and plan their marches—
Thus in firm confederation
    Time's old rancor to forget.

Thus it was that by the lake-side
Grew another sylvan dwelling,
With its rugged beams and bastions,
With its porch and palisading,
And its gnarled and·twisted gateways,
    Planned by cunning architect;
And the gaunt arms of the cedars
Twining lovingly about it,
    Sought its portals to protect
From the fierce brigands of tempest
That across the unsheltered prairie
    Many a hapless home had wrecked.

And the maid with cheeks of carmine,
And with scarlet berries twining
    'Mong the tangles of her hair,
Sat and sang from morn till evening—
Sang the songs the winds had taught her
    In their rushing near and far;
Beading moccasins of buckskin
    For her bridegroom chief to wear.

*   *   *   *   *   *

One long day in blossoming spring-time,
When the willows by the courses

Put their feathery plumage on,
And the heron to his fishing
    By the reedy lake had come;
And the blue-bird screamed and chattered
To the partridge and the plover,
    In the deep woods, all alone—

Then the pale-faced captain, loosening
From their cove his painted paddles,
· Tied his crimson sash about him,
And unto the Sachem's daughter
    Gallant waved his *au revoir;*
Saying, "when the full moon rideth
Through the furthermost horizon,
She shall touch with silver pencil
    Lightly my returning oar."

But the "dark moon," black and sullen,
Glowered upon the tasseling larches,
    Bending o'er the shaw-shaw's roost;
And upon the ghostly hemlocks,
Standing there like surpliced hermits,
    Wondrous apparitions tossed;
And the waiting bride grew weary—
Weary watching through her lattice
    By the tangling grape-vines crossed;
Weary calling to the waters,—
"Wherefore bring ye not my lover

On your faithless bosom thrust?"
Weary conjuring the south wind,—
"Speed! O speed his skiff ot birch-wood,
    Stranded on some lonesome coast."

While the south-wind, never heeding,
Rollicked past in wild gyrations;
And the regiment of waters,
    Trampling onward toward the shore,
Gave no answer to her questions—
    Muttering on as heretofore;
Left the lonely watcher sitting
On her braided mat of rushes,
    Pensive by her cabin door.

Long she sat and watched the billows
On their battle fields contending;
Watched the clouds that lay at anchor
    Like some‾calm-bestranded fleet,
Till her eyes flashed strange and brightly
With a sudden inspiration,
    And with swift descending feet
Down she fluttered to the sedges—
Where her red canoe lay floating
    Since the last year's sun had set;
Seized the paddle, idly lying
    'Mong the waves that scold and fret—

Pushing out upon the waters
In her rocking birchwood cradle,
      Like a nautilus adrift;
Laughing at the crest of surges
That the tumbling billows left,
As they bounded from their cavern
      Of the rock's unbolted crypt.

From his roof-tree screamed the eagle—
Screamed the war-bird of the Sachems;
Hailed the dark-eyed Sachem's daughter
      Passing 'neath his household bough;
She with laughing challenge dared him
O'er the boisterous lake to guide her—
      Fold his great wings on her prow;
But the bird of battle only
Fluttered o'er his noisy broodlings,
Flapped his broad plumes from his eyrie;
And adown th' turbulent current
      Watched the fearless maiden go.

Down thus o'er her childhood's waters
Steered the wayward navigator,
Talking to the sleepy sturgeon
      On the sunny surges stretched,—
"Know'st thou where my chief has anchored?
Where his paddles 'mong the rushes
      Rippling beams of sunlight catch?

I have called him through the forests
And the solitary places,
   But my calls no echo fetch."

Past the death-mounds of the warriors,
Where the wild-rice shook and shivered,
Where the crane and heron brooded .
   'Mid the ghosts of brave and chief;
Past the ancient "tree of council,"
Where the princes of the nation
And the forest lords had gathered,
   From the prairie, coast and cliff,—

Still undaunted and unfearing,
Down the river of the Foxes
   Swept the fearless lake-shore naiad;
Swept this daughter of the warriors,
   Blanching not, nor yet afraid
At the distant muttering thunder
   By the wrathful rapids made—
As they plunged and leaped and circled,
Galloping like battling armies
   Leaping from their ambuscade;
Though their voices shook the thickets
   With a shivering of dread.

Still, like wild-bird in the tempest
   Chirping to the winds of death,
3

Sat the slender sun-browned pilot
　　Listning to the war beneath;
Planting well her painted paddles
On the rocks that frowned and jutted,
　　Where the billows boil and seethe.

With her dark eye glancing upward
Came a whispered invocation—
　　Came the snatches of a prayer,
Mingling with the roar of surges
　　Tossed upon the quivering air,—

"Spirit of the waters, hear me,
From thy place among the ledges,
Where the weendigoes * at midnight
　　Walk the limestone rocks and prate;
From thy seat, where, through the ages,
　　Thou hast watched the doors of fate,
Lay thy hand upon my paddles—
O'er the dangerous rapids guide me,
　　Through the river's rocky gate."

From her neck she tossed the wampum,
　　Dashed her bracelets in the wave;
Laughed to see the spirit-fingers,
Hid beneath the writhing billows,

* Ghosts.

Clutching at the gift she gave;
Saying to her tiny frigate,—
"O, my skiff, be staunch and brave;
Safely bear the Sachem's daughter
　　Through the floods that scold and rave."

Then her quivering paddle loosening
From the rock that 'scarce had held it,
On a great broad-shouldered billow
　　Swept she down the wild abyss;
Where the weird imps of the torrent
　　Turbulently roar and hiss,
Bounding like a stormy petrel
　　Down the watery precipice.

Sheets of foam lay all about her,
　　Shrouds of surge white demons wrought;
Yet the frail bark bounded o'er them—
Bounded on with fearless plunges,
　　As by spirit pinions caught,
As by spirit hands defended,
Though the water-ghouls, awakened,
　　Madly for their captive fought.

On and on, the elfin frigate
Flitted by past cove and cascade,
Till the April sun, o'erwearied,
Watching from his cloud-capt bulwarks

O'er the errant voyager,
Sought his couch within the westland,
    'Neath the sombrous belt of fir—
Roused upon the upper headlands
    Whole battalions of the stars;
Bid them hang their beacon torches
From the arches of the heavens,
    Lighting ship-wrecked mariners.

And the Indian maid Hopekah,
Floating where the waves grew calmer,
Saw the footsteps of the Sachems
In the milky way above her,
    Through the firmament bestrewed,
Saw the ancient chiefs, her fathers,
Glancing on her from their lodges,
    Through the caravans of cloud;
Saw their tomahawks gleam and glisten
    Brightly through the evening shroud,
And her grateful salutation
    Chanted to them clear and loud,—

"From the gateways of the Westland,
Smile upon me, O, my fathers!
Smile upon your wandering daughter
    Out upon the floods alone;
Where the great trees nod above·her,
And the strange birds scream about her.

` And the night winds sob and moan;
See, I come,
Down the rapid river gliding,
All alone!

Light for me within the doorways
Of your misty spirit-lodges
All your glittering rows of torches;
Guide me where my lover waits—
Where he ties his sash of crimson,
Plumes his cap with heron's feathers,
Somewhere near the river's gates;
Stand and guide me
With your fitful spirit-lanterns
Where he waits."

And the night-owl heard the chorus,
And the plashing of her paddles,
From his lonely hemlock roost:
And he answered with an echo
Like the shrieking of a ghost,—
"Who is this that rides at nightfall,
Over ledge and rock and rapid,
Like some boatman tempest-tossed?"

And the simple maiden answered,—
"It is I, the Sachem's daughter!
And I seek my pale-browed captain

Where the Frenchman ties his ships;
Where the big guns of his thunder,
Down within the bay-shore harbor,
   Safe our great White Father keeps."

Past the Mission of the Fathers,
Where the great Kakaulin rushes
   Through its barricades of pine;
Where the bittersweet and hemlock
O'er the solitary temples
   Of the wilderness might twine;
This lone Winnebago maiden,
   Passing by the leafy shrine—
Marked upon her brow the symbol
   And the sacred countersign
Of the cross her husband worshipped,
   Seal of mysteries divine.

There were flambeaux flaring brightly
At the old fort by the bay-shore,
And the tall masts spread their colors
   As the shallop bounded in;
And the awe-struck traders staring
   At the maid with face serene,
Swore by all the gods of thunder
   That a specter they had seen;
But the graceful wanderer, tying

'Mong the weeds her skiff of birch-wood,
　Told her quest with princely mien,—
"Know ye of the chief De Kaury?
He who wears the heron's feathers;
Tell me where his camp-fire flickers
　'Mong the clumps of evergreen."

And the traders pointed yonder
To a brave ship bearing outward,
With her flags and canvas flying
　In the freshening evening gale—
Where, upon the taffrail standing,
Towered the sturdy chief, her husband,
　Reefing in the straining sail;
When his quick eye, glancing downward
Through the glittering row of torches,
　On the Sachem's daughter fell. ·

With one bound the deck he measured,
And the seamen in the rigging
　Gazed in mute astonishment
When the stalwart trading captain,
　Late so stern and arrogant,
In his strong arms clasped her to him;
　Though a blank bewilderment
Sat upon his earnest features—
　Knit his brow in wonder bent.

"Wherefore thus, my lake-shore maiden,
From thy nest among the sedges
Hast thou ventured thus unguarded
    Through the solitary pass—
Hast thou dared those dangerous waters
    Dashing through the wilderness?
Fear'st thou not the ghosts that wander
    Lonesome lakes and wild morass,
That thus for a recreant lover
Thou should'st dare the imps of danger
    In a race so hazardous?

Not again, my wild sea-eaglet,
Will I trust thy wayward impulse;
Not again will risk thy pinions,
Like thine own free waves untethered;
    Yonder on my goodly sloop
I will hold thee for a captive.
And if, through the great sea-water, *
With its giant rocks o'erhanging,
Where the bear and panther harbor,
    'Mong their dens our sail should swoop;
Thou shalt try thy arrow on them,
Make the great bear of the mountains
    Down beside thy feet to stoop;

* Lake Superior.

Fashion thee a robe of ermine,
Steal thy cloak from off the panther
    Or the spotted antelope.

So the tall sloop from the harbor
    Sailing at the wind's behest,
With her gusty sheets unfolded,
Like a stately cormorant flapping
    Her white pinions in the mist;
Flew before the coastland breezes,
    Swept in majesty the waste.

And the corn was in the tassel,
And the cardinal flower was blooming,
E'er the sail of bold De Kaury
    Saw those ancient cliffs again—
E'er his eaglet to her eyrie
    By the Winnebago came,
Back to weave her mats of grasses,
    Resting from her long campaign.

And e'er scarlet grew the sumach,
And the yellow-mantled beeches
    Showered with gold the forest ways,
And the cricket of the autumn
    Chirped through long September days,
Filling up the misty spaces
    With his antiquated lays,—

One long day a birch-bark cradle,
Deftly wove and quaintly beaded,
　　Hung beside the wigwam door;
And Hopekah 'mid her broideries
　　Sat beside it on the floor,
Singing weird-like songs and ditties,
Untranscribed by scald or linguist,
　　To the waif thus tossed ashore,—

　　　*　　　　　*　　　　　*

"Ah, my little mountain eagle,
Little wandering unfledged eagle,
Straying to my couch of grass;
Ah, my wonderful Chougarah, *
　　　All the stars,
　From beyond their evening bars
　Light those glorious eyes of thine,
　　　Baby mine!

　Rock and swing,
To thy birchen cradle cling,
　　Warrior mine!
Little panther from the cliff-tops
　　Where the hemlocks climb."

　* Chougarah De Kaury, afterwards head chief of the Winnebagoes.

Thus the dusky forest princess
Sang away the shimmering summer,
With the wondrous cradle swinging
    From the gnarled oak's rugged bough;
Till the winter marching quickly
On his snow-shoes stalked the forest,
    Tracked the morass through and through;
But among his bear-skin curtains,
In his scarlet blanket swaddled,
    Still the little warrior grew—
Chirruping in wondrous language,
He had learned across the mountains,
    To his father's retinue.

Thus the summer and the winter
Came with bloom, and blast, and blossom,
To the Winnebago lakeshore—
    Came with hurrying sandals on;
And a squad of little warriors
By the Frenchman's vine-wreathed doorway
    Sat and chattered in the sun;
Chattered to the muttering billows
    Trooping shoreward, one by one.

And the brown squaws husked the maize-ears,
And the hunters shot their arrows,
And the braves adown the war-path
    Marched in long battalions grim;

And the moons, all uneventful,
  Rode with rounded crescent in.

But the hoarse, deep-throated billows
Vaguely muttered to the cedars
Of a hurricane that, sweeping
  O'er the big sea-water bar,
Filled the great French Father's coast-line
  With the thunderings of war;
From the scabbard that had sheathed them
  Woke the sword and scimetar.

Often now, with arms close folded,
Gazing o'er the stretch of waters
  Where so long had been his home,—
Sat the bronzed and stalwart captain,
Sat and pondered through the watches
  Of the midnight, all alone!
Self-absorbed and meditative,
As though tangled problems weighing—
Problems that his soul had measured
  By a fierce comparison.

Thus, one evening, sitting rigid,
With his bent brows stern and knotted,
Heard he not the step beside him,
  Till a gentle hand was laid
Soothing on the locks that clustering

O'er his damp brow swept and strayed;
And a timid voice, beseeching,
Spoke with language half afraid,—

"Why sits my chief alone upon the shore,
With the great waves all strangled at his feet?
Why talks he to the west-wind scudding o'er,
Why strains his eye where the great waters meet?"

And the listening chief made answer,
Dashing back the heavy tresses
From his damp and pallid forehead,—

"Hark! heard I not the belching of the guns
From the dim Heights of Abraham afar?
Was it the echo of the cannon's boom
That swept across the lake with sudden jar?"

"Rest thee, my chief! the Spirit of the Storm
Rumbles and mutters through yon beetling cliff,
Waking the braves that slumber further down;
Saw'st not their tomahawks through the darkness
lift? *

* The Indian believes that the spirits of the dead warriors visit the earth in the tempest, and the lightnings are the
flashing of their tomahawks.

"My fathers were all warriors; moons on moons
  Have left them sleeping 'neath the limestone ledge;
But when the storms are out they walk the earth,
  And visit then their olden heritage.

Thy rest shall be with theirs, my pale-browed chief!
  My father's bow shall slumber by thy side;
The ancient wampum round thy neck be hung,
  And near thee sleep thy dusky forest bride.

But wherefore strains so bodingly thine eye
  Beyond the forest-crested lake away?
Why fiercely throb the veins upon thy brow,
  Laid on my shoulder, hot and restlessly?

Dost thou not love me? Does thy spirit pine
  For fairer forms the big sea-water o'er—
For softer voice than hers who chants for thee
  Beneath the shadow of her wigwam door?"

"It is because I love thee that my soul
  Starts with a sudden pang this twilight hour;
Daughter of chiefs! the love I gave to thee
  Wakes up within me with a stronger power.

For thee, and those young warriors of thine,
  Fain would I rest me on this sylvan strand;

But hark! the Great far Spirit calls to me
  In tones of thunder, from my fatherland.

I hear the blare of trumpets on the breeze—
  The tramp of war-steeds o'er the far off waves;
And loud, across the sweep of yonder seas
  The winds are calling from my fathers' graves.

Unloose thy arms, maid of the Western wild!
  In pity turn from me those tearful eyes—
E'er thy young eaglets waken at the morn
  My sail must point afar toward Eastern skies."

"And wilt thou leave me? must I sit and pine
  Upon the mat before my lone lodge door—
Till the leaves crimson on the hanging vine,
  And the snow-drifts creep the dismal forests o'er?

And must I watch the clouds go sailing by
  Like braves upon the war-path, one by one;
And know not if thy spirit pass me nigh,
  Bound for the gateway of the setting sun?"

"Nay, by my soul! the spring–time's gentle rays
  Shall find me folded in thy arms again;
Unless the direful fates of battle-days
  Shall leave me sleeping on the trampled plain.

If such a fate the battle-gods decree,—
If woe the dark portentous clouds betide,
This wampum string a messenger shall bear
   Through mountain wilds—o'er billows deep and
   wide,—

Through pathless prairies and through tamarack
   swamp,
Until it reach thy vine-encircled door;
And thou shalt wear it proudly for my sake,
   Although thy warrior should return no more.

And now, farewell! the lightning's lurid glare
   Shall light my shallop o'er the tossing lake;
Daughter of Chiefs! thy gushing tears forbear!
   Wear thy grief proudly for thy warrior's sake.

Dark beauty of the wild! farewell, farewell!
   Swift swaths of foam my venturous bark shall make,
Watch well the dim horizon, faint and far,
   Till o'er the western wave my sail shall break."

   Down the solitary passes,
   Through the shadows swept the oarsman—
   Through the dim, unanswering shadows,
      Closing round him still and mute;
   Through the highways of the waters,

Whose rough billows, uncombatant,
  Cared not now to hold dispute,
But around the painted paddles'
  Tossed and toyed irresolute.

And a pensive voluntary
  Swept the surge with fitful gush,
Gathering in its incantations
  Echos through the solemn hush,—

THE INDIAN BRIDE'S SONG TO HER DEPARTING
WARRIOR.

"Walk lightly o'er the waters,
O spirit of the tempest!
Light warily thy torches,
  Till my lover's light canoe
Flits through the Eastern gateway
To the city of his fathers—
To the land that first was trodden
  By the mighty Manitou.

Rein in thy war-steeds tramping
O'er the solitary mountains—
The mountains grand and ghostly,
  Where the buried Sachems march;
And sheath their flashing tomahawks
That have rent the clouds asunder,
4

As they kindle at the midnight
   Their flaming battle-torch.

For my pale-browed chief rides proudly,
And my hero skims the billow
In his tiny skiff of birchwood,
   Like a swan from out the reeds;
May the ancient warriors lead him
To the distant fields of battle,
And fill his locks with war-plumes
   Where the prostrate foeman bleeds."

*   *   *   *   *   *

In a palpitating silence,
In a mournful, misty silence,
Drooped the pale and wasted summer,
   Sobbing her wan life away;
With the crimson lights upon her,
Soft as from dim castle windows
   O'er the mountain's boundary.

All the day the squirrel chattered;
All the eve the brown quail brooded;
All the night the wa-wa nestled
   'Mong the rushes and the sedge;
And the beaver at his bulwarks
   Toiled along the river ledge.

And the mists grew deeper, thicker,
  On the forests round about,
Till the birds had ceased to twitter;
And the ancient hunters watching
  From their craggy, weird redoubt,
Said, "The spirits of the sachems
  In their misty gear are out,
Kindling up their smoky watch-fires
  On their old forgotten route."

Sobbingly the west wind wandered,
And the lone poetic pine-trees
  Told their mournful prophecy;
And the yellow mantled beeches
With the zephyrs that had flirted,
  Swaying in their ecstasy,
Swirled and shook, and swung their branches,
  As in smothered mutiny;
And the wild-goose from her rushes
With vociferous racket stirring,
  Toward the southward hasted by.

Then the winter's wild battalions
Rushing from their Arctic dungeons,
  Held their headlong tournament;
Burst like lions of the desert
  On the shivering forests bent.

Every warrior fled before them,
With his spear and bow unbended;
Every tall, majestic heron,
 To some sheltering cove had flown;
And the stern, unyielding cedars,
 Held the war-path, all alone!

Would ye know where hid my Princess,
Through the silent days that followed—
Where her little brace of warriors
 Crooned their infant dialogue?
Look within the antlered doorway,
Where the counterpanes of bear-skin,
Spotted cat, and fawn, and badger,
 Form full many a royal rug.

There, in all the lore she treasured
From the legends of her people—
In the wild traditions taught her
 By the prophets of her tribe;
From the books their father left her,
Sought she slowly to transcribe
 To those scions of alien races,
Myths, and creeds, and lore historic,
 Wrought in wondrous narrative.

Regent of a weird dominion,
Whose rude scepter down the winters

Of the years was swiftly traveling,
And whose diadems barbaric,
　　Toward her unaccustomed brow
With the moons were quickly hasting
　　Her dark tresses to bestrew;
With her woman's heart bestranded
On the shores of two horizons,
　　Watching all the tides that flow,
Questioning all the winds that wander
Through the far and unknown spaces,
　　Rushing wildly to and fro;
Questioning with a dim foreboding,—
"Bring ye tears, or bring ye gladness,
　　In your midnight mutterings low?"

*　　*　　*　　*　　*　　*

One bright morn the forests sparkled,
　　Sheathed in icy coats of mail;
Brilliant in their stolen diamonds—
　　Robed in shimmering tissues pale,
Like a frozen bride enshrouded
　　In her glittering wedding veil.

And across the cold mosaic
Of the icy lake there hurried
One who on his snow-shoes traveled
　　Leagues and leagues of drifted waste,
Coming to the Sachem's doorway,

With a hasty step, and fast,
Halting with unsteady purpose,
    And with brow that turned aghast—
Speaking in a husky whisper
    And his eye with tears o'ercast,—

"Know ye whose this string of wampum—
Whose this tasseled sash of crimson?"
    Asked he in a faltering speech;
"Yonder, o'er the blue St. Lawrence,
Where the towering Heights of Abram
    Frowning o'er the broad gulf reach,
There my friend and comrade faltered,
Wounded by a British saber;
Like a scathed and shivered oak-tree
    Prone he lay upon the beach!"

*   *   *   *   *   *

Have ye ever felt the silence
Of the great woods, deep and solemn,
When the fury of the whirlwind
    Through its peaceful crypts has rushed;
And the cedars and the pine trees
    Down beneath its hoof lie crushed?
So that morn of frosty splendor
Looked the cabin by the lake-side,
    In its desolation hushed!

Prostrate, on her mat of rushes,
Lay the chieftain's darling, panting
Like a wild gazelle that, wounded,
    Hides her 'mong the tangled brake;
Moaning to the distant waters
Of the great gulf to the eastward,—
"Bring me back my chief, my husband!
From the dead, or from the living—
In his plumes, or in his death-shroud,
Bring him, O ye winds of winter,
    On your wrestling pinions back!"

But the west-wind, sobbing, moaning,
Wandered on across the mountains;
And the shrouded cedars muttering
    Passionate dirges doled and spent;
And the stern-browed warriors, passing,
Stealthy near that threshold bent,
Bowed their dusky heads in silence,—
Wrapped their arms upon their bosoms
    In a silent discontent.

O, those days that came uncalled for!
O, those nights that went uncounted!
    Stretched to centuries e'er they crept;
Can the years whose fearful chasms
Stand unbridged where last we leaped them,
    With no spar to intercept—

Can the tinge of sunshine gild them,—
Looking back o'er life's horizon,—
Gild those awful precipices
　　Whence our tottering feet escaped?
*　　　*　　　*　　　*　　　*　　　　*
O'er his daughter bent the Sachem,
Bent the old man, tempest-stricken;
But her sad eye on distance
　　Fixed as though she heard him not:
"Daughter of my dead Nehotah,
Rouse the sleeping fire within thee;
Thou must raise a race of warriors,
Thou must wear thy father's wampum,
Thou must sit and lead the councils;
　　Rouse thee! though all unforgot
Be the grief that rends thy spirit;
Let the daughter of the Sachems
Bow with dauntless acquiescence
　　To the fate the gods allot."

Slowly, as a soul that travels
Through illimitable spaces,
　　To the bounds of other spheres,
Wanders back to life's rough highways—
　　To its torture and its tears;
So that stricken spirit backward
Stole across the wide abysses
　　Days had lengthened into years,—

Looked into the stormy faces
Of the moons that lay before her;
Laid aside the sash of crimson
    That her chief was wont to tie;
Laid aside the heron's feathers,
    Gazing long and reverently;
Laid aside the songs she caroled
In the Indian-summer weather
    Of those golden days gone by;
Stood again before her people
    Garbed in sorrow's majesty.

And the errant winds have told me
How her form was seen at midnight
Gazing o'er the stormy billows,
    Far, so far away beyond;
Where the clouds lay piled like fleeces
    In the distances profound.

How her voice grew low and tender,
How her hand brought aid and soothing
    To the homes of grief and want;
How she sat within the doorway
Of the grey-haired chief, her father—
    Watched his step wax slow and faint;
Till one night across the hill-tops
Glowed the torches of the Sachems,
    Through the silvery clouds aslant;

And the old man, whispering feebly,
Bade them rein his favorite war-horse—
Bade them bring his bow and arrows,
Bade them start him on his journey
    Up the path his fathers went.

How through long dark years he sat there *
Like a "skeleton in armor,"
Holding in his bony fingers
Broidered reins that dropped in pieces,
    Halting on that weary march;
While his mute and obdurate mustang
Bore him never nigh or nearer
To the gateway of the Sachems—
    To the cloudland's outmost porch.

How, beneath the Tree of Council, †
On the old historic lake-shore
By the stormy Winnebago,
Sat my Princess 'mong the warriors,
    Queen amid those dusky knights;
With the wampum of her father,
    And his war-plumes well bedight;
And while flamed and crackled round her

---

* Buried on his war-horse.

† The old council tree still stands on the eastern shore of
Lake Winnebago, near the city of Neenah.

Boughs of pine and spruce and tamarack,
This the charge she gave her chieftains
    On that weird heroic night,—

"Brothers, when the pale-face wanders
To the wilds our fathers left us,
Sheath your arrows in their quiver,
    Hide your tomahawks in the grass;
Meet ye not in feud, as foemen,
    In the solitary pass:
But with hands outstretched, as children
Of the Great far Spirit yonder;
Hark! he sends you on the south-wind
    Messages of love and peace!

Bid the white man plant his corn-fields,
Sail his big ships on your waters:
    Smoke with him the calumet;
For across the distant mountains
Must his star up the horizon
    Ride the heavens, when yours has set!"

So when to the vine-wreathed doorway
Of the widowed Sachem's daughter,
Strayed one morn a bearded stranger *
From the far land of the sunrise,

---

* Carver.

Craving space within her door;
Called she forth her trusted hunters—
Called she forth her men of council;
Bade them give the pale-faced traveler
Room and welcome in their lodges,
Bid them spread for him a banquet
    On the old lake's sandy floor—
Greet with open hands and hearty
    The white chief's ambassador.

*   *   *   *   *   *

Black and smouldering lie the embers
On the shores of Winnebago,
Quenched by storms and winds of ages,
    By the tempest and the flood;
Gone the old ancestral cedars
    By the breezy lake that stood—
Gone the eagle from his hemlocks,
Gone the panther from his covert,
Gone the sachems from their camp-fires,
    Leagues along the upper road.

And Hopekah, through the shadows
Long since heard her lover calling
    Through the unexplored expanse;
Long since wrapped her robes about her,
Seeking for him through the boundaries
    Of the earth's circumference.

And the old lake, still and solemn,
Ever since has sung her dirges—
Ever since a miserere
    Droned for her at evening-tide;
Would ye hear its incantations?
Stand with me upon its beaches
When the tempests toss their surges,
    Rave and wrestle in their pride;
You shall see the ancient lovers,
You shall hear the painted paddles,
Keeping time-strokes with the cycles
    As adown the waves they glide.

                 1876.

RUNES FROM THE FOREST.

RUNES FROM THE FOREST.

THE SACHEM'S GHOST.

'Twas a weird and elfish midnight,
When the tempest's wings unfold;
And the knell of distant storm-bells
Across the old lake tolled—
The old lake Winnebago,
That for centuries had rolled.

The angry waves washed over,
And the frantic waves, unchained,
Came leaping ever shoreward,
Unfettered and unreined
Like the mustang from the pampas,
That no lasso ever tamed.

Beneath an ancient cedar,
With its scraggy arms outflung—
With the mosses from its branches
Like whitened scalp-locks hung,
Stood a grey old ghostly warrior—
5

A warrior gaunt and grim;
And he stood and stared upon the waves,
And the waves stared back on him
With a look of questioning wonder,
And a grim defiant stare,
As they tossed their foam unsparing
'Mong the tangles of his hair.

Then the warrior broke the pauses
Between the tempest's screech,
With his withered arms raised upward,
And with wild, disjointed speech:
"Oh, wind-rocked Winnebago,
Know'st thou not who treads thy shore?
Know'st not old Yellow Thunder,
Who in the days of yore
Led his feathered hosts to battle
Through the cedars green and hoar—
The strong, unbending cedars,
By the hurricane swept o'er?"

"Knowest not he whose arrows
Brought the eagle from his perch?
Who lighted up the council-fires
With blazing hemlock torch,
And called the chiefs and sachems
Back from their outward march,

With their tomahawks and deer-skins,
And their red canoes of birch ?"

"Oh, wind-rocked Winnebago,
Thou art traitor to thy trust !
We bid thee with thy billows guard
Our fathers' slumbering dust;
We bid thee drive the pale-face back
From off our burial mounds,
When we should wander far away
In the happy hunting grounds.

But to-night upon the stretches
Of thy forest-guarded strand,
In the lonely midnight watches,
Back to my father's land—
Back to the shores stamped over
With the footsteps of my band,
I come, and come to curse thee
Above my father's graves;
And to leave my ban upon the sands
Where wash thy traitorous waves."

"Where are the braves I left thee,
An hundred thousand strong,
With their hatchets gleaming proudly
And their wampum bravely strung ?

They answer not my war-cry
The olden beach along !

There stands with hoary branches
The Sachem's council-tree, *
Unscathed, as when the heron
Built 'neath it silently;
But the chiefs who smoked the peace-pipe
Like fallen forests lie,
With not a hand to wave aloft
The fire-brand to the sky—
And not a wigwam standing
Thy restless waters nigh !

Oh, wind-rocked Winnebago,
With the same old fearless sweep;
With the lashing of thy surges
And thy thunderous voices deep,—
Where are thy sun-browned children
I left for thee to keep,
Whose moccasined feet along thy banks
At eve were wont to creep ?
Gone, with the crane and curlew !
Gone where the west-winds sleep !

* Still standing on the west shore of the lake.

And the white man's foot comes marching
With a strong and steady tramp,
Far down to meet thy billows
Where our braves were wont to camp;
And we count their sweeping cities
By the midnight glaring lamp,
That flares where lay our rice-fields
And tamarack guarded swamp.

His iron-horse* snorts defiant
Our burial mounds across,
Where erst thy treacherous waters
Were wont their spray to toss;
Where we laid our sires and foemen
In that moon of fearful loss,
When the life-blood of our heroes
Stained deep the fern and moss.

We bid thee keep them sacred
When the Winnebagoes' trail
, Should point where flies the wild-goose,
And where the white clouds sail;
When the dirges of our war-tribes
Should load each passing gale.

* A branch of railroad now runs directly through the "Hill of the Dead," on the shores of Lake Winnebago, where the Foxes, Sacs and Winnebagoes met in battle.

Oh, wind-rocked Winnebago,
`For thy lightly-broken faith,
I will haunt thee in the tempest
Like some fierce and angry wraith;
I will mow thy stately cedars,
I will blast thy lordly pines:
And my torch shall scorch thy prairies
In the goodly harvest times.

I have leagued me with the whirlwind,
And when ye hear his tread
Come trampling down the hemlocks,
And the tall oaks overhead,—
When he lashes thee to fury,
Till thy billows boil and rage,
Thou shalt see my shape upon thy shores
Sworn endless war to wage;
To haunt like an avenging sprite
My father's heritage !"

GREAT MICHIGAN AND HER CITA-
DELS.

O wrathful, storm-scathed Michigan ! whose billows
   Sweep out thy beacon-lights from cliff and tower,—
Rocking thy rugged mariners as on the pillows
   Of giant ocean waves, that send their roar

Through listening continents; we hear thy voices,—
   Talking in thunders, o'er thy surges rolled—
With answering soul, that shivers or rejoices
   When thou thy carnivals of tempests hold.

The ancient eagle long has left her cradle,
   Her storm-rocked cradle on the hemlock's bough;
The blue-winged heron stoops not now to dabble
   In wild-rice swamp, skirting thy shores below.

The ghosts of brave and sachem with their torches
   Flaring, no more at midnight haunt the cliffs;
Along thy sandy beach no warrior marches,
   No feathered clansman, and no beaded chiefs.

Gone! all are gone! Another race and people
   Wander thy shores and rear thy granite piles

In towering bastions, or aspiring steeples,
  That lift their heads in pompous pride the while.

Hushing thy lordly waves to silence never,
  Quenching their echoes neither day or night,   ·
Thine old barbaric roar sweeps on forever—
  Unawed, unhushed; though frowning ramparts
    fright

Thine ancient harbors, and great hulks, o'ersweeping
  Thy noisy waves, float proudly out and on;
Forgetful that the dungeons 'neath thee sleeping
  May yet unbar their gates and gulf them down.

Strong citadels are perched on thy dominion !
  To eastward and to westward, lo ! they rise !
And the swift bird, pluming at morn her pinion,
  May not outsweep them e'er the day-light dies.   ·

Bulwarks of empire, that the sun in setting
  Far o'er unfathomed seas shall never bound;
Whose landmarks—mountain peak and crag forget-
    ting—
  Shall stretch away through desert wastes profound.

Thy Sabbath bells ring out their evening vesper,
  From shore to shore, across thy broad domain;

Flinging their anthems to the soft southwester,
Bidding the forests wake their bold refrain.

We mind us of a Sabbath, gone to story,
When o'er thy leagues a burning cyclone swept,
Wrapping the frightened heavens in awesome glory,
Bursting upon the citadel that slept

Down on thy southern verge, whose midnight watches
Were broke with wild alarms, and wails that rushed,
Along thy pebbly strand and misty reaches;
With crash of tower and rampart that lay crushed

In awful ruin; while in flaming surges
Swept the mad hurricane, with fierce wings tossed,
Above the queenly city's utmost verges,
Impatient for the fiery holocaust!

And when the moon looked down at midnight
watches,
Grim specters glared through dome and marble
hall;
And all was still as where the bittern hatches
Or where the cormorant stands sentinel.

Quick years have fled, and from those costly ashes
Rise sculptured column, massive architrave,

Firm bedded in the rock thy billow washes,—
Ordained, perhaps, the centuries to outbrave.

Roar on! old Michigan, in thy defiance!
And guard the cities sleeping at thy feet;
And bind the hurricanes in thine alliance
O'er thy tempestuous shores that rave and beat.

And when another race with noise and clatter
Ride through the portals that we rear to-day,
Guard sacredly the "death-places" we scatter
Upon thy hill-tops, when we pass away!

Sept., 1878.

———

BURIED IN HIS WAR-PLUMES.*

"Warriors," the tawny Sachem said,
"The sun goes down in the bloody west,
With his crimson blanket o'er him spread,
Like a chieftain robing himself for rest.
Mine too, goes down! o'er the smoky hills

* To-pe-kah, a magnificent-looking Indian, six feet high,
shot by the Chippewas for killing some of their tribe. Before
death he distributed his robes and ornaments among them,
reserving only his eagle's feathers won in battle.

I hear the Great far Spirit call!
'To-pe-kah,' he says, 'take the wa-wa's trail,
Along where those clouds of purple fall,
Through the gates of the evening urge thy steed
To the plains where the hungry bison feed,
And the antelope tends unscared her young;
Where the great war-eagle
His eyrie makes,
And the heron broods in the quiet lakes;
Hark! they call thee on,
The Sachems of old in belt and plume!'

"So, warriors, here at your feet I fling
My white elk robe and blanket of blue,
And my beaded pouch, and my wampum string,
And my mantle all fringed with scalp-locks too.
But my eagle's plumes, that I won in the fight,
Shall slumber with me; and when I cross
The war-trail up in the clouds to-night,
They shall wave in my long hair, as I pass
Through the gateways beyond in the crimson light;
And the Great far Spirit, from off his seat
On the hurricane cloud, shall hurry to greet
The hero in,—and the Sachems shall say,—
' Open the gates of the morning wide:
The gates of the morning,
Gold and red,

To the brave that on his war-steed rides,
With his eagle-feathers of white and grey.'

"So brothers, my favorite mustang call,
From the fields where the blue-topped grasses bend;
He hath borne me oft in the chase and fight,
And his fearless step has outstripped the wind;
Ye shall gear him proudly, and gear him well—
In his crimson girths and his feathered crest—
For I and my steed in the pale moon's light
Must gallop far and fast to-night,
For leagues and leagues, toward the misty west!
Ye shall hear the clank of his hoof-beats ring
Through the blue arch yonder; and when we tread
The thunder-cloud, ye shall hear aloft
The roll of my footfalls echoing,
And the downward gleam of my tomahawk's flash
On the fiery tips of the lightning's wing; *
And when the wind in the cedar-tops
Talks hoarsely, and shakes their boughs amain,
Ye shall know that the ancient warriors ride
Abreast o'er their far off trails again.

"Let me sing my death-song—here among
The ancient hemlocks that sob and bow,—

* The Indian believes that the lightning is the flashing of
tomahawks of the Sachems.

They are grieving because in the clouds beyond
To-pe-kah's sun is waning low;
Because his place will be still and lone
At evening around the council-fire:
Warriors, the sun is almost down,
Point well your arrows, braves, and fire!
But first let me bind the eagle's plumes
Fast on my brow, lest the west wind's breath,
That sweeps o'er the happy hunting grounds,
Should waft them away o'er the prairie heath.
The night-owl calls, with his loud too-hoo;
My sun is down! Warriors, I go
Up the shining trail of the wa-wa's track!
Call me not back! Call me not back!"

OLD YELLOW THUNDER'S RIDE.*

There was tempest in the waters;
And like the roll of guns
From some dismantled fortress,
The thunder rattled on;

* This old veteran, whose portrait hangs in the State
Historical Society's gallery, died in 1874, on the Wisconsin
river, above Portage. He was over one hundred years old,
and quite a hero in his day; he was chief of the Winnebagoes, then a powerful tribe.

And from unbolted caverns
  Leaped the disfranchised waves,
That writhed, and foamed, and tumbled,
  Down to their billowy graves.

'Twas a carnival of tempest,
  And the frightened forest broods
Hied them quickly to their coverts
  In the leafy solitudes;   ·
But the great grey-headed eagle,
  Peering from her nesting tree
Where the gnarled limbs of the cedars
  Told many a century—

Sat and laughed, across the waters,
  At the wild winds' maddened roar,
As it bowed the olden hemlocks
  And the ancient sycamore;
Sat and laughed, and screamed defiance
  To the billows as they tore
From their limestone-grated dungeons,
  On old Winnebago's shore.

From out his lodge of driftwood
  The Sachem of the lake
Answered the strange bird's weird-like screech
  With spectral echo back,—
"Bird of the storm, I greet thee;

In my painted bark canoe
I will talk with thee upon the waves,
And the mighty Manitou,

When his footstep passes by us,
Will bid the mad waves keep
The skiff of Yellow Thunder,
Out alone upon the deep."

Wrapping his deer-skin round him,
In his brawny hand he clenched
His painted paddle, while the foam
His feathered scalp-locks drenched;
And like the sea-bound nautilus
Breasting the billow's crest,
Rode the skiff of Yellow Thunder
On the angry waters cast.

O'er the muttering lake rebounding
Sped silently his craft,
Beneath the ancient cedars,
Where the eagle sat and laughed;
Past the mounds where lay and slumbered
'Mid the tempest and the calm,
Braves and warriors, all unnumbered,
Listening to the old lake's psalm.

Still unsilenced rolled the thunder,
Still unpaled the lightning swept;

But that frail boat, unaffrighted,
  O'er the wrathful billows leaped—
Down the river of the Foxes,
  Where the mad waves gallop on
Like war-steeds to the contest,
  When the battle has begun.

With his paddle yet unflinching
  Firmly planted in the rock,
Stood erect old Yellow Thunder,
  Dauntless as the forest oak.

"Spirit of the storm," he muttered,
"Give me strength and give me prowess;
Strength to ford these noisy waters
  With my fragile skiff of bark;
Chain thy fitful forks of lightning—
Talk in whispers to the billows,
  Bid them to thy footfalls hark;
O'er these wild tempestuous rapids
  Guide me e'er the night grows dark!"

"See, I give thee strings of wampum,
Scarlet cloth and heron's feathers;
Shining beads and painted arrows
  In the foaming floods I fling;
Pilot well, and pilot surely,
And my little bark of birch-wood
  Safely to my wigwam bring!"

Then his quivering paddle loosening,
  Dashed he o'er the foaming verge,
And his staunch craft floated onward
  Like a curlew on the surge;
And the forests, as he passed them,
  Rocking wildly on their thrones,
Bowed in homage to the warrior
  In his crest of eagle's plumes.

*   *   *   *   *   *

There were stars upon the waters
  When that red canoe of birch,
Still upon the topmost billow
  Holding yet its fearless perch,
Down the river of the Foxes
  Halted, as the moon rode in,
Where the great Kaukalin rushes
  Mid its clumps of evergreen.

And the night-owl in the hemlock
  Screamed aloft his loud too-hoo,
As that phantom bark of birchwood
  Through the rapids glided through;
And the torches from the wigwams,
  O'er the tossing surges sent,
To their bands of swarthy sentinels
  A weirdish glitter lent.
6

"Brothers," said the storm-drenched sachem,
"Give me food and give me blankets;
Light the peace-pipe at the embers,
    Safe my painted paddles keep;
I have seen the mighty rapids,
Ridden on the steeds of tempest—
Whispered with the Great far Spirit
    Out upon the noisy deep;
Spread the bearskin near the fire-log
Till the morning lights the forests,
For the Winnebago Sachem
    Waxeth weary! let him sleep!"

                                    1876.

––––––

THE GATHERING OF THE SACHEMS.

Crimson and gold, in the forests old,
The maples their royal flags unrolled,
And the sun went down in the smoky west,
Like a warrior robing himself for rest;
    And far in the cedars, loud and shrill,
    Piped up the noisy whip-poor-will,
    At the hush of eve when all was still.

Far over the lake, just flushed with flame,
The muffled murmur of paddles came;

And the coves, where the rustling wild-rice grew,
Were flecked with many a bark canoe:
 And the snake-brake tangled along the shore
 With moccasined feet was trampled o'er,
  When the Sachems came that autumn day
  To the gorgeous woods, in their bravery.

Beneath the council tree * that sprung
To its mossy throne when the earth was young;
Where their grey-haired sires their war-talk gave
By the Winnebago's tossing wave;
 Whose boughs through the hurricanes had stood
 Monarchs of that grim solitude;
  Then floating up as the red sun set,
  The chiefs and sachems in council met.

Fearlessly out rung their welcoming shout,
 Waking the cedars round about;
And the heron up from the brake and sedge
Flew far to the distant limestone ledge;
 And the wild loon laughed in his stormy glee
 As he gazed on the weird-like company.

Up from the rocks of the tumbling Fox,
Whose wave at the sweeping ages mocks;

.

* The Council-tree still standing on the shores of lake
Winnebago.

Where the hoot-owl, startled from off his perch,
. Flew past the prows of their skiffs of birch:
   Up from the Red-stone-quarries south—
   From the dark "Death's Door," at the grim lake's
     mouth;
     From the lone Wisconsin's pine-girt shores,
     Where the panther screams and the eagle soars.

   From the beach where the crested white gulls
     sweep,
   Where old Michigan rocketh her dead to sleep;
     From the Spirit-lake with its beetling steeps,
     Where the shadow of ancient legends creeps;
From the grass-girt mounds where the braves were
    held,
By the loon and the heron sentineled,—
     All gaily geared in their belt and plume,
     The chiefs to the lake-side council come.

   And the hemlocks sage, that for many an age
   Had guarded their fathers' heritage,
Bowed low their helmets, just touched with flame,
To welcome the warriors as they came;
     And the beeches from out their cloister old
     Showered down on their pathway a flood of gold,
     On the sandy shore where the old lake rolled.

   Then quickly among the pine boughs crashed
   The ringing hatchet, and all aghast

Stood the startled woods, as the blaze went up
Far over the gloomy cedar's top,
  Waking the specters that glower and lurk
  Betwixt the gloaming and the mirk.

With his bear-skin cloak from the knotted oak
Swaying and swinging as he spoke,
And his brown neck hung with the wampum strings,
And the circlet of mottled eagles' wings—
  With brow where the lurking thunder slept,
  Old Grizzly Bear from his lair had crept;
    And the words like wrangling billows broke
    From the old chief's lips, while thus he spoke,—

"Wherefore, O braves, with your bows unbent,
Sit ye and glower o'er the embers spent,—
  Counting the feathers that ye took
  From the eagle's nest upon the rock?
When yonder, upon the southward trail,—
Where, singly and still as the creeping snail,
  Our braves through the slumbering forests stole,—
    Last night, with their torches all aflare,
    A *pale-faced host*, in their battle-gear,
    Stole past the haunts of the sleeping bear?

'Tis well that 'neath your idle feet
Lie the ancient braves in their quiet sleep,
Or these solemn woods would blaze to-night

With spear and tomahawk, glistening bright,
And the war-whoop echo from height to height!
  Will ye barter for strings of painted beads
  The ground where the Great far Spirit treads,
Where his footsteps sleep in the rocks and stones,
And his whispers are heard in the old lake's moans?
  Strike, lest ye waken his ire and rage,
  And from your ancient heritage
He sweep you away with his hurricane breath,
Like the grasses that shrivel upon the heath."
   *   *   *   *   *   *
Crimson to-day, in the forests old,
  Have the maples their royal banners rolled;
And the ancient elm, by the old lake's shore,
Stands as it stood in the days of yore—
  All decked in its regal robes of flame,
  As when that elfish caravan
  Of forest sachems to council came,
  Beyond the hill-tops and over the plain.

But no heron's plumes, 'mid its branches lost,
  Flutter aloft 'neath the eagle's roost;
No painted war-club is raised aloft
O'er the noisy waves that have surged and chafed:
  The hoary cedars have bowed and bent
  To the winds in their stormy tournament.
    And the wa-wa's nest in the beds of rice,
    And the curlew haunting the precipice,

And the loon amid the flags and sedge,
That crept to the old lake's sandy edge,—
And the braves that in their wild array,
With pomp and savage heraldy
Flocked to their council—where are they?

1876.

WISCONSIN'S FIRST LEGISLATURE.

No frescoed corridors or fluted column
Waited their gaze, who through the tamarack wild,
From prairie's marge, from dim woods deep and sol-
emn,
Where scarce the sunshine through the hemlocks
smiled—

Toiled their lone way, blazing the trees behind them;
Breaking the branches of the birch and fir,
To mark their trail when eve's long shades should
find them
Where never settler's lamp burned faint and far.

Rugged their bear-skin coats—their painted snow-
shoon
Made lordly strides along the forests bare;

Where the tall pines, like great masts on the ocean,
  Stood up all scarred with fire and tempest's war.

The panther glared on them with fiery eye-ball
  From out the dim ravines, so hushed and black;
And the hoot-owl, with plumage rough and piebald,
  Screamed to the gray wolf prowling o'er their
    track.

Yet dauntlessly through wild and wold they traversed,
  Their rifles o'er their sturdy shoulder tossed,
Massing their arguments with which to waken
  Those pristine halls, whose jagged rafters crossed,

And then re-crossed in marvelous architecture,
  Worthy a cruder age, so long gone by;
Filling the soul with fanciful conjecture
  What era claimed their rude priority.

Staunch souls, and brave were they whose rugged
    cohorts
  Marshalled themselves upon the rough-hewn floors;
The wind-racked forum, where they met in conclave,
  The people's choice—the land's ambassadors.

Souls stern and strong, hewn from the ancient quar-
    ries,
  Whence were hewn giants in the elder days;

Firm as the iron-wood in their lordly forests;
  Whose words, when waked, the pliant mass could
    sway—

As marsh-grass in the rushing tempest shaken,
  Or maize before the prairie whirlwind bent;
Whose voice had wondrous power to rouse and
    waken
  Long echoes, sweeping on, omnipotent.

'Twas thus, with strokes clear as from their own axes,
  Were cleft the bastions of the sturdy west;
Whose granite corner-stone still firmer waxes,
  Though surge and surf its rocky front resist.

Patient they traced the marge of coming cities,
  Bounding the wilderness with bolt and bar:
And where the cat-bird chimed her dolorous ditties,
  Hearing the hum of noisy marts afar.

Mosses and grasses over them are lying,
  Dismantled forests shivered at their feet;
But every wind across the old tracks flying
  In solemn reverence their names repeat!

THE OLD NORTHWESTERN BRAVES.

They slumber well! The nightmare of the ages
  Breaks not their dream, who in their birchen shroud
Sleep on unwaked,—the forest's vanished sages
  Who walked the hills with valiant step, and proud.

Still slumber they within the dim mausoleum
  Of greenwood minsters, 'neath their chanceled
    aisles,
Lulled by the anthems bursting deep and solemn—
  The anthem of the waves, that all the while,

Through the far yesterdays, so long departed,
  Have kept their watches by the olden shore,
Though the rude warriors—stern and iron-hearted—
  To their wild surgings answer back no more.

No more the clash of glistening tomahawks waken
  The screeching owl from off her nestling tree;
No more the war-whoop through the brush and
    bracken
  Calls up the forest's wild artillery.

No more with torch and flambeau down the river
  Dances at eventide the light canoe;

No more the sassafras and sumach quiver
With moccasined footsteps lightly flitting through.

Their ruths and wrongs the tides have hushed to
    quiet:
Their stormy chronicles about them sleep;
And the untethered winds in their mad riot
    Sink soft and low as o'er their graves they sweep.

O, weird and silent sepulchres, unmarbled,
    Must ye be dumb and voiceless to the last?
Shall no staunch oak—no song-bird that hath warbled
    Adown the war-trails of the misty past—

Sing us your idyls, dim and untranslated—
    The wild heroic idyls passed away?
For which the patient years so long have waited,
    The tangled legends of the elder day?

Unreverently we dare not tread the heather
    Beneath whose bloom unsceptered princes lie;
Our shoes from off our feet we lay, and wander
    Like awe-struck pilgrims, to a cloister nigh.

Guard well! ye golden elms and sombrous birches,
    The ancient clansmen sleeping at your feet;
Whose whitened bones the restless lake-wave
    bleaches,
    Whose rhymes and runes the wintry winds repeat.

1877.

SONS OF THE SACHEMS.

Gone from our hills are tawny chief and clansman, .
  Gone from our forests battle-ax and spear;
Gone from our lake-sides birchen lodge and wigwam,
  With winding hunter's trail in ambush near.

Gone from their feudal halls among the beeches,
  Their lone cathedrals where the torrents rush;
Their hunting-grounds along the pathless prairies
  Where silence reigns with an eternal hush.

We ask the stars to point us to their war-trails,
  We ask the winds to tell us where they sleep;
But only tempest answers unto tempest,
  And drones their dirge in measures hoarse and
    deep.

Lords of the wilds! whose dynasty lies shivered
  Beneath the civilizers' ruthless tread,
Whose archives 'neath our battlements lie buried,
  Whose monuments beneath our feet are laid.   .

Their deeds have passed from off the page of story:
  Only their names we call by stream and grot;
Only their ghosts we see all gray and hoary,
  But feathered chief and sachem answer not.

But now their sons—like lonely cedars rising—
   Among the desolate cliffs, by sobbing waves,—
Ask for a standing-place where they may linger
   Beside the ashes of their father's graves.

They cross with halting feet our marble thresholds,
   And ask for foot-room in our classic halls,
Where their impassioned souls, so late awakened,
   May read earth's lore, so dim and mystical.

Shall we not fling wide open on their hinges
   The cloistered doors, locked to the forest sage?
And o'er the wrecks of generations vanished
   Mete out to them our higher heritage?

Scions of hierarchies long lost and withered,
   Children of nations faded in the mist;
Across the mossy thresholds of the ages,
   By motley tribes trod with such hurrying haste—

We clasp your hands, brown with the forest sunsets,
   On which the Manitou his signet pressed,
And bid you carve your name among the granites
   That crown the hill-tops of your ancient west.

                                          1877.

LORDS OF THE WILDERNESS.

Come from your hiding-place, lords oɪ the wilder-
    ness!
Come from your fortresses hidden by brake;
Where in the solitude hatches the thunder-bird,
    Where the white swan skimmeth over the lake.

Come as ye will, all unbraided your scalp-locks!
    Tangled the wampum-strings, carelessly strung;
Loose o'er your shoulders the mantle of wolf-skin,
    Bristling the quivers ye carried so long.

Sachem and Sagamore, dash through the gulches:
    File through the pass in the lonely bayou;
Stand where the waterfall leaps o'er the precipice,
    Where walks at midnight the great Manitou!

Stand where your tomahawk shall flash in the light-
    ning,
Marshal your cohorts the boulders among;
Read us the runes of unchronicled ages,
    When your warriors were brave and the cedars
        were young.

Long have we asked of the tempest to tell us
　　Legends of dynasties dumb 'neath the mold;
Come from your hiding-place, Sachem and Sagamore,
　　Read us the records of nations of old.

Sept., 1877.

THE PRE-HISTORIC GRAVES.

Tread reverently the old historic graves
　　That sleep forgotten in the creeping moss,
Where the ancestral oak its branches waves
　　And sleepless winds of centuries blow across.

There rest the braves of ages that are past,
　　Each with his heron plumes upon his brow;
His bended bow laid near him 'neath the grass,
　　And many an autumn's leaves above him now.

Lords of a race whose footsteps from the soil
　　The hurricanes of time sweep fast away;
Gone like their fallen cedars, that erewhile
　　Guarded the forests in the ancient day.

Sleeping along their war-trails, that we tread
　　Unthinkingly to-day, with hurrying feet:
Sleeping beneath the cities that have spread
　　Their granite piles through many a dusty street—

Above their bleaching bones, whitening beside
   The wild vociferating lake or prairie's verge;
They slumber on, whatever fate betide:
   Unwaked, unheeding, through the storm and surge.

Then reverent tread the old historic graves
   That sleep forgotten 'neath the creeping moss,
Where the ancestral oak its branches waves
   And sleepless winds of centuries blow across.

TREASURE CITIES OF THE WEST.

Beneath the hoof-beats of our steeds, whose clatter
   Rings over parapet and prairie sod,
Lie the weird citadels the mold has buried—
   The Herculaneums that the ancients trod!

Wrapt in the swathings of the crumbling cycles,
   Shrouded in cerements that no hand can lift;
We wade with wildered feet above the portals
   Where leaves of centuries idly toss and drift.

We rear our granite piles above the bastions
   Where forest lords once sate in royal state,

And drive our iron-racers o'er the death-place—
The lone sarcophagus where Sachems wait!*

We desecrate with sacrilegious fingers
The archives of the nations lost in mist:
The chronicles the Manitou has left us
Of his lost children scattered o'er the waste.

How will the nations still to come absolve us?
How will the sages of the yet to be
Rain curses on the race whose ruthless clutches
Have stolen tithes from time's weird legacy!

O Goths and Vandals, of an age unreverent!
Who gather ingots on the shrines of kings
And vend their shrouds in alien marts exulting,
And count the bags of zechins that they bring.

The hurricane that mows the works of ages
May one day whistle through *your* corridors,
And dance among the ramparts ye have builded,
And laugh among your marble sepulchres.

---

* Through the beautiful "Hill of the Dead," on the west
shore of Lake Winnebago, has actually been cut the track of
the Central Railroad. This was one of the most picturesque
nooks the state contained, and should have been held sacred
for posterity through all generations.

7

Then touch with tender hands the mouldy remnants
  That lie upon the thresholds of the past,
Whose architects have long since trod the pathway
  Toward the lodges of the shadowy west.

Jan. 14, 1877.

THE SHIPS OF ASTOR.

Landing at the old fort, Green Bay, Wis.

Shivered and torn came the ships of the sailor,
  Down from the rent, jagged peaks of the north;
Flags rudely tattered by wind or by hail, or
  Shivered by hurricanes marshalling forth.

Up in the taffrail, with grey locks a-bleaching,
  Stood the old trader in his wolf-skin bedight;
Shrill from the westland the wild winds came screech-
    ing,
  Rattling the rigging in angry despite. .

"Heave to, my men," said the stalwart commander,
  "Let go the anchor, there! reef in the sail!"
Thankful ye ride not the rough sea to-morrow,
  Out in the teeth of this threatening gale.

So by the old fort, down there on the bay-shore,
Floated the rent flags, all tattered and seamed,
While from their nests flew the tall crane and curlew,
Up from the crags where the red lightning
gleamed.

Filled was the old hulk with skins and with peltries,
Robbed from the crag-tops the great lakes beyond;
From the tenantless forests, the lone pathless moun-
tains,
And the ice-bergs that slept in the silence profound.

Down through the hatchways and up in the rigging,
Clambered the red-painted Sachems and chiefs;
On their brown shoulders the panther skins bringing,
Borne down the streams in their lithe birchwood
skiffs.

Tawny-cheeked princesses cautiously wander,
Wonderingly, over the storm-weathered craft;
Brilliant in necklace of carmine and amber,
Peering like sylphs from the awnings abaft.

And the old log-hewn fort, from its loop-holes and
bastions,
Down there on the outermost shore of the bay,
Looks down in its state like some palace barbaric,
Which holds at its portals a weird holiday.

SPARE YE THE FOREST TREES.

Spare ye the forest trees,
  With shreds of dynasties about their tangled roots—
Those guardsmen of the shattered centuries,
  Whose broad green banner o'er their ruin floats.

The hieroglyphics of the ages past
  Are written on their shaggy coat of bark,
Though neither scald, nor seer from out the waste,
  Reads us their superscription, dim and dark.

Spare ye the sentinels that guard the graves
  Of buried clansmen,—battle-ax and bow
Lie moulding 'neath their canopy of leaves,
  While footfalls of the nations come and go.·

The Shasters of the people gone to dust
  Sleep at their feet; the birchen coffin-lid,
Through which their gnarled and knotted roots are
      thrust,
  Holds jealously the secrets of the dead.

Left by the hurricane, whose hurrying feet
  Swept like a demon through the forest pass,

They stand where snow-drifts weave their winding-
    sheet,
Or summer winds drop flowers amid the grass.

And when the piles our pigmy fingers rear
    Lie leveled like the ant-hills o'er the plain,
Still to the winds their foreheads they shall bare
    Like sceptered monarchs of their wide domain.

Then spare the forest trees, that watch and wait
    The coming cycles, with their gaze intent;
Nor dare with sacrilegious hands to desecrate
    Those hoary records of the Omnipotent.

                             Sept., 1877.

THE OLD PIONEERS.

Brave, dauntless hearts, whose clear unclouded vision
    Looked boldly out across the untraversed waste,
And mapped their cities in the pathless forests,
    And by the lake-shores, limitless and vast.

Men of broad souls, who, wearied with the chafing
    With narrow minds, and creeds so circumscribed—
Built for themselves a lineage 'mong the prairies,
    On the staunch oaks their heraldries inscribed;

And through the arid summers and the winters
  Toiled for the generations yet to come,
And flecked the hills with oak-ribbed schools and
    temples,
  And filled the valleys with their vine-wreathed
    homes.

The frost is on their locks to-day, and feebly
  Droop their tall forms, so strong in days of yore;
We meet them on the highways as we wander
  Like stalwart pines by hurricanes swept o'er.

The marts they planned, the cities they have builded,
  Loom o'er their heads, and now their footsteps
    trend
Toward those silent cities on the hill-side,
  Whose mournful cypress to the sad winds bend.

Brave, loyal hearts! their monuments are chiseled
  On every hill–top where the sunsets fall;
Their obelisks are carved the broad state over,
  From humble cot to marbled capital.

And jealously we watch the scathing winters
  That toy too rudely with their locks of snow,
And wonder if the land in long to–morrows
  Can fill their places when they shall be laid low.

                                        1877.

WINTER ON THE FOX RIVER.

Old Winter sits throned on the beautiful Fox,
With his white robes of ermine strewed over the rocks;
And the voice of his winds, whistling over the waves,
Like the song of a witch from her hollow oak caves.

The old trees bowed lowly their beautiful head,
As the king of the tempest in majesty sped;
And the sered leaves came down in a torrent of gold
To carpet a path for the monarch of old.

The moss-channeled brook that roll'd down from the
      hill
And over the bank where the beech-nut tree fell,
Stopped short in its gamboling and murmured no more,
When the foot of the tyrant fell harsh on its shore.

But lo! thou pale ghoul from the white frosted sea,
There's a wild wave that yieldeth not even to thee:
There's a stream that defies thee, and mocks with its
      roar
The spells thou hast flung o'er its beautiful shore.

Boast, boast if thou wilt of thy trophies of pride,
On the floods, where the ice-reefs and snow-moun-
    tains glide,
Where the blanched mast stands up like a sprite
    'mong the waves,
And the Polar ghosts sport o'er the mariner's graves.

But know that the flood of the red-man shall pay
No homage to thee, or thy tempest to-day,
For still, in derision, its rapids shall roar
Untamed and unfettered as ever before:
To mock thee enthroned in thy pomp on its shore.

1863.

BATTLE DAYS.

BATTLE DAYS.

MISSING.

Darling, come back! the crimson setting sun
  Tints the red sumach in the forest way;
And thro' the tangled paths the fading leaves
  Of royal maple wantonly do stray.

The breath of early spring-time has gone by;
  The summer roses faded 'neath our feet—
And soon the wintry winds, unfeelingly,
  O'er our accustomed haunts will toss and beat.

How long! how long! across those southern hills
  With pallid cheeks and wet eyes must we look
To catch the shadow of thy manly form
  That from our arms the angry war-drum took.

Alas! the dreary dungeon's heavy door
  Shuts out the hopes that wing their way to thee,
And slowly crawl along the days and hours,
  And then, within that prison-pen they say

In some lone midnight watch they laid thee down—
　Our darling and our strength—and life grew black,
And hearts sobbed on and broke since thou wert gone!
　Gone from our love! no, never to come back.

We hear the wild bells ring along the shore— ·
　We see the old flag sweep the hills again;
We watch the hosts returning home—but o'er
　Our souls there sweeps a wild tumultuous pain.

Thy step is not with theirs—thy smile no more
　Will sweetly light the household hearth at eve;
We hear the stately horseman passing by,
　But we, alas! no welcoming shout can give.

O winds, that rock those southern pines at night,
　Will ye not tell us where our darling lies?
Far through these blinding tears we strain our sight;
　Speak to us of him in your hushabys.

But the wild winds from out the southern pines
　Send forth their answer, "Out in the beyond—
Soothed by a softer cadence than our rhymes—
　Your darling wanders, the still streams among!

His voice takes up the psalm he learned on earth—
　Learned through the darker mystery of woe;
And if ye listen well, its seraph note
　May cheer your path till ye are called to go."

STARVED IN HIS CELL.

O, wind of the west! sad wind of the west!
  Why brought ye not to me the prayers of my dar-
    ling?
They tell me they laid his young brow to its rest
  Long ago, long ago! when the red leaves were fall-
    ing;
And now come the days of the storm and the snow,
        And yonder, I know,
The white drifts above him are mocking my woe!

Starved! Starved in his cell! how I listened and
  waited,
  At morn, and at midnight, for whispers to come;
How I watched through the casement for some star
  belated,
  To guide through the darkness my precious one
    home;
But now, his gaunt features, all whitened and wan,
        Stare at me alone!
Heaven light the dark paths for the desolate one!

O, wind of the west! wild wind of the west!
  Why brought ye not to me my darling's last kisses?
I know that he left to your faithless behest

Fond words for his loved ones, and earnest caresses;
Sweet memories, that might through the saddened
  heart glow!
        But all that I know
Is,—he died in his cell! O, my God, is it so?

———

THE RETURN OF THE OLD BATTLE FLAGS.

From the land of the everglades homeward we bring
  them,
  The storm-battered flags of the stripes and the
    stars,
And proudly aloft o'er the hill-tops we fling them—
  The old flags we followed with prayers and with
    tears.

Long moons have gone down since the bugle-blast
  quavered
  Wide over the prairie and down by the sea,
And the fields have been reaped and the harvests
    been gathered,
  And the weeds seeded over the graves of the free.

Battalions of brave ones have gone to their slumber,
  The hoarse drums have beat and the mourning
    bells tolled;

The cannon has waked up the coast with its thunders,
And the blaze of the cities toward heaven hath been
rolled.

But the Captain of Hosts laid his hand to the battle,
And the foemen were still as the spccters of night;
And hushed was their boasting and silenced their rat-
tle,
And dumb were their legions with sudden affright.

And now o'ẻr the mountains, all hallowed and hoary,
We fling to the winds the torn flags of the free;
They shall live in our hearts—they shall linger in
story,
As long as the storm-winds surge over the sea.

DIRGE OF THE YEAR 1865.

Bells of the North! toll forth, toll forth!
In sad and solemn strain,
For thc brave whose sleep is long and deep,
And who never shall waken again!

Dead, in the coastland along by the sea,
And dead in the everglade swamp;
Dead, in the forest and mountain gorge,

And down in the dungeon's damp!
While alone in their tears
The weary must sit by their hearths to-night,
And gaze down the desolate years;
Bells of the North! toll forth, toll forth!
And mingle your dirge with theirs!

Bells of the North! ring out, ring out,
In a pean loud and shrill—
Through the mighty heart of the stricken land
Bid gladder pulses thrill,
For not in vain lies the crimson stain
On the snow-drifts, white and still.

The sob that the broad plains echo forth
Far out on the midnight air,
Some other day shall to anthems swell
For the listening seas to hear;
And the banner float o'er the mountain-top,
With never a missing star,—
With never a shackle to rattle and ring
Its curses on our ear.

The watching centuries stand and wait
With their massive gates unswung,
Till the new year bring its records in;
And the crusaders have sung
Above the storm and the cannonade,

A nation's freedom song;
For with blood and tears must the right prevail
Since ever the earth was young!

With blanching cheek and with clasping hands
Through the midnight long we say,—
"Father, who guided the destinies
Of the nations passed away,
Roll back the wild tempestuous tides
That o'ersweep our shores,—and may
The watchman yonder, upon the tower,
Foretell a peaceful day!"

UNCROWNED HEROES OF THE CENTURY.

Have ye forgotten how the tremulous shiver
Swept through the land that panting summer's day,
When traitors ranged their cohorts on our coastland,
Filling our frightened shores with wild dismay?

Have ye forgotten how our braves, uprising
From cairn and cliff, from forest cot and hall,
Sprang to the echo of the bugle's calling
To wrest their clutch from fort and arsenal?

8

How, when the red sun, through the west departing,
　Stayed pityingly their bayonet-tops to gild,
They lay in winnowed rows along the furrows,
　Like swaths of grain upon the harvest-field?

How, when the cannon's throat had done its roaring,
　And battered flags swept homeward, one by one,
From Sumter, and from Moultrie's sea-washed bas-
　　tion,
　From Lookout Mountain and from Lexington,—

When to the roll-call, waking hill and valley,
　That o'er the crags and cliff-tops wildly smote,　•
There answered but a handful of our legions,
　While many through the silence answered not!

And now their battered forms upon life's highways
　We meet, amid the glitter and the show;
With prison-stories writ upon their faces
　And battle-histories furrowed on their brow.

O nation, prosperous and well beloved,
　Must these stand halting at the city gate—
Striving with palsied hand and fever-stricken
　To wrest a morsel from the grasp of fate?

While men with stunted souls, and craven-hearted,
　March to the cushioned seats and take their place,

And count the nation's coin, and wear her baubles,
  Her chains of gold, her ermine and her lace?

And those who bore the people's ragged banners
  Crowd at your thresholds, as the crowds go by,
And shiver in the tempests of December,
  Or scorch beneath the sultry August sky.

Your chiseled heroes mock the scornful heavens—
  Your granite giants rise in awful state;
But 'mong the weeds that at their base lie gathered
  The "uncrowned heroes" of the century wait!
                                    1876.

OUR PEACE-OFFERING.

Lincoln, assassinated April 14, 1865.

We were busy hanging the banners
  From the steeple-height and dome—
Hushed was the cannonading,
  And the ranks were marching home;
Marching along through the highways,
  Through pathways long and dim,
To the notes of the drum and bugle,
  As they struck the nation's hymn.

We had sealed the cause of freedom
  With our hearts' blood in the strife—
We had writ it in the mountain gorge
  And on the beetling cliff;
We had shouted it from the hill-tops,
  And along the coastland's sweep,
Till the loud waves echoed it back again
  With their thunderous voices deep.

And the stately ships in the harbor
  Hung their torn flags from the mast,
All rent and scarred by the shot and shell
  That had whistled through on the blast.

We had waded through wild Decembers
  In the trenches or the marsh,
We had buried our frozen comrades
  By the midnight's ghostly torch;
We had pined in the Southern dungeons
  Where the famine left its trace,
And now in the gladsome April days
  Came God's sweet gift of PEACE!

Peace! how the children sang it
  On the green hill-sides the while!
How the organ rolled its anthems
  Down the dim cathedral aisle;
How the mother wept as she spoke it

By the graves of her noble slain,—
"There is *peace* in the land, my darlings,
    And ye have not died in vain!"

But down 'mid the land's rejoicing,
    From citadel and tower
Came the echo of hoarse bells tolling,
    At the solemn midnight hour;
And we looked aghast to the Eastland,
    And we gazed afar to the West,
"What woe betides the land," we said,
    "What specter outrides the blast?"

We gazed in each other's faces,
    All blanched with a strange affright.—
"Why toll the bells through the darkness
    O'er the joyous land to-night?"
We waited with eager questioning,
    And peered down the silent street;
What horror smites the people
    That they stand with palsied feet?

And a grey-haired sire made answer
    As he beat his lone patrol,
"The land is *fatherless* to-night!
    'Tis meet the bells should toll!"

· UNSCEPTERED.

Abraham Lincoln, assassinated April 14, 1865..

No statelier soul than thine sleeps 'neath the gloom
  Of old Westminster, with its hundred aisles;
No nobler peer or prince of power claims room
  'Neath frescoed arches, where the sun reçoils.

No kinglier form than thine lies swathed in pride
  Beneath the cerements of the ages gone;
With granite obelisks above their head,
  Forgotten hieroglyphics on their stone.

The stamp of royal lineage marked thy brow,
  So worn with care, so fraught with problems deep;
So haunted with a nation's destinies,
  Stealing like specters through thy harassed sleep.

Yet strong to meet the hazards of the day—
  To dare the angry cyclones as they beat
All through the fearful night, relentlessly,
  Shoreward and seaward, past thy stormy seat.

We heard the booming cannon rake the hills,
  We saw our routed armies strew the plain;

We watched our blazing ships whelmed in the flood,
  Our banners riddled in the leaden rain;

And then with tear-dimmed eyes we turned to thee—
  With thy wan face and mute,firm lips, struck dumb,
Reading with patient face the augury
  Writ on the walls of time; while there alone,

Upon thy silent watch-tower, pacing slow,
  Counting the nation's heart-throbs as they fell
Upon the palpitating silence low,
  Thy footfalls echoed to the midnight bell.

O great, strong heart, perched on thy storm-rent cliff,
  To watch the nation's throes of agony!
O brave, true hand, to whom the pen was given
  That bade the oppressed ones of the Lord go free!

We ask no scepter for thy peerless brow,
  No heraldries of proud historic line;
Thy meed of fame earth's chroniclers shall write,
  And freedmen's tears shall gem each burning line!

No need for sculptors' aid to mark thy sleep;
  The unerring chisel of the century
Shall carve thy name in letters broad and deep
  Upon the cliff-tops of eternity!

March 4th, 1878.

PEACE!

From the blue-bannered hills to the cliffs of the ocean
 The peace-flag, majestic, floats over the main,
And across the broad plains in a joyous commotion
 Battalions of brave ones flock homeward again.

The glad land breaks out in a thankful ovation
 To Him who rides on through the earthquake and
 storm,
For the blast of her nostrils hath risen and shaken
 The foe; and they scattered like mists of the morn.

The sad years have passed with their wild cannon-
 ading,
 The thunders of battle have died on the· breeze;
The tri-colored banner is floating triumphant
 'Mid scepters and hierarchies over the seas.

Across the blue hills comes the flash of the bayonet,
 The echo of trumpets, the roll of the drum;
And the broad Westland pours, from her prairies and
 forests,
 A welcoming hymn to her veterans home.

MISCELLANEOUS POEMS.

ALONG THE MISSISSIPPI.

Summer days of 1878.

The land had gathered its harvests,
  The golden fruit lay piled
In the glowing orchards, while in the fields,
  Where the swarthy laborers toiled—

The cotton whitened like fleeces
  The wide plantation o'er,
And the rice creaked on its heavy stalk
  By the rich bayous near the shore.

But through those days of summer,
  Through those sultry August noons—
Where from the mangrove and the pine
  The oriole piped his tunes,

Came an awesome shadow creeping
  Along the river's marge,

And sat like a sheeted ghost of doom
'Mong the cities on its verge.

And strong men, hushed with terror,
   Asked 'neath their bated breath,
"Will the grim destroyer walk the land?
   Shall we clasp pale hands with Death?"

Still hotter and sultrier grew the days,
   And still the specter sate
Unasked, unbidden, by our hearths;
   And at his cruel feet

Dropped down our beautiful darlings—
   And we buried them from our sight;
And the glorious bloom of those autumn days
   Hid not our woe and blight.

The rich man fell in his palace,
   The poor man by his hearth;
The giddy reveler in his halls
   In the gay saloons of mirth.

The priest sank down at the altar,
   The bride by the marriage bed,
And scarce enough were left at their posts
   To carry out the dead.

And often in lonely outskirts,
  Where the poor their woes outbrave,
Sank mothers with only little ones
  To hollow their lonely grave.

All through the silent watches
  Of the night, there came and went
The rumbling wheels of the death-carts,
  Like hungry ogres sent

· To sweep the halls of the stricken land;
  While we stood with haggard eyes
Waiting for the burning lips to close,
  And hush their agonies.

'Twas then than the silent cities
  Their awesome sabbaths kept,
And the grass grew up on the marble stair;
  'Mid fluted columns crept

The noisome weeds, and the watch-dog
  Howled on the threshold stone;
While only the cricket chirped on the hearth,
  Untenanted and alone!

How longingly, as we panted
  In that charnel-house of death,
We watched for God's coming angels,
  Stealing with noiseless feet

Through the doleful streets, whose echoes
  Came as from mouldy tombs;
While the dead lay there uncoffined,
  Forgotten in ghostly homes.

For God's sweet coming angels
  We waited night and day,
Through those long and endless watches,
  When our brown locks turned to grey.

For their step across the threshold
  And their footsteps on the sand,
As they came with help and mercy
  To the plague-bestricken land.

*   *   *   *   *   *

The land has gathered her harvests!
  The reaper's sheaves lie cast
On the bare, unsodded hill-sides;
  Our noblest and our best!

On the bare, unsodded hill-sides
  The wealth of our homes is laid;
Heaven send us the russet autumn leaves
  To cover up our dead!

SCORCHED IN THE TUNNEL.

The moonlight fell aslant the floor
  Upon that soft October eve,
The crimsoning vines about my door
  That through the autumn's long reprieve
  Their tangles stayed to interweave,
Just sobbed a little to the breeze—
'The warm southwester, as it swept
Across the prairie,—while below
  The noisy mart its Sabbath kept.

My little ones with wondering eyes
  Watched the red moon come sailing up,
And painting on the arid skies
  With burning brush her horoscope,
While tangled in her slanting rays
  The home-bound ships to harbor rode—
Mowing their swath across the lake,
That into foaming furrows brake,
  All flushed as with a trail of blood.

One tiny head upon my arm
  Had dropped its silken showers of gold,
While I sat marveling if the spheres

In all their rounds such wealth could hold;
When quick across the stifling air
The great bell rang from out the tower,
And clang and clash rose deafeningly
Upon the solemn Sabbath hour—
Rocking the steeples with their roar,
And seeming to the stars to pour
Rash prayers in their wild agony.

I brushed aback the tangling vines
And gazed the leafy labyrinth through,
Where the great city held her shrine
'Mid granite fortresses, and lo!
A fiery cyclone in the East
Jeered mockingly the harvest moon,
And laughing at the frightened bells
Clanging so widely out of tune,
Strode leaping on from roof to roof;
Mounting the battlements, to scoff
At all the frantic crowds below,
Like coast-waves surging to and fro.

I clasped my babes, for even then
The hot breath flushed my pallid cheek,
Borne onward by the hurricanes
That galloped past me fast and fleet;
The little burnished head of gold
Upon my arm hung heavily;

Great God! how should I launch my babes
  Afloat upon that fiery sea?

Beneath my casement surging on
  As though by cloven demons chased,
The multitude rushed madly down
  To where the turbid river washed.
"Make for the tunnels!" rose the cry—
  The scorching billows onward tossed;
And 'mid the crowd tumultuously
My unresisting babes and I
  Dashed to the fiery holocaust!

The heated stones beneath our feet
  Burned like some lurid crater's bed,
And scrolls of flame went hissing past
  Fresh havoc on their path to spread;
The snorting steeds neighed wildly back
  To the mad winds that screeched and tore,
And fainting mothers in their paths
  Sank with the little ones they bore;
And still those awful bells of doom
  Rolled dirges trom their granite tower!

We fought our blinding way along
  Amid that hell of smoke and glare,
Still beating back with frantic hands
  The sullen specters of despair,
  9

Still asking mercy of the flames
  That darted on us unaware,—
Till where the murky tunnel opes
  Its caverns 'neath the river's plash,
With one wild, desperate bound for life,
  The surging thousands wildly crash!

Packed in a writhing mass, we stood
  Like felons in a convict ship;
And "Water, water!" rose the cry,
  In tortured tones from lip to lip,—
And overhead the river rolled,
  The boiling river—smit with flame;
And underneath the panting crowd,
  Asking a draught that never came.
When downward borne, across the crypt,
A sheet of fire its barriers leaped,
And on the helpless ranks it swept;
  The mothers and the little ones,
  Begging compassion of the stones!

I strove, my God! how long, how long!
  I strove my clinging babes to shield,—
To shield amid the trampling throng,
  Rushing like horsemen to the field;
Till down beneath their iron feet
  They crushed me like a quivering reed,
And then the light went out,—but still

That fierce crowd trampling overhead!
They tell me that as from the dead
They rescued me.   Alas! I weep
To think they did not let me sleep;
    For when my eyes unclosed again,
That little burnished head of gold
Lay in its beauty—stifled, cold!
Dropped from my faint arm's circling fold!

———

LOST ON THE REEFS.

On the wreck of the Schiller, lost April, 1875.

There was mirth in the stately cabin
    Of that grand old ship of the line,
As she ploughed her furrows, long and deep,
    Across the trackless brine;
And the crimson curtains shivered
    With the dancers' noiseless tread,
And the great wheels writhing among the foam
    Their snowy pathway made.

She was bound for the glorious Rhineland,
    That storied land of old,
With strength and beauty within her keep
    And ingots within her hold.

And wherefore should doubt o'ershadow,
  Or omens of evil be,
'When no thunder growled in the midnight sky
  And no hurricane threatened a-lee,—
And the old ship's bell rang strong and well
  From her bulwark over the sea?
    O, the sea! the marvelous sea!
Man spreadeth the sails and stretcheth the shrouds
    Of his royal argosy;
But the mighty God, he keeps the keys
    Of the citadel under the sea!

And what if the fog was heavy,
  And what if the clouds grew thick?
Her binnacle-lights still gleamed aloft
  Across her oaken deck.
And they toasted the far-off Fatherland,
  With its castles tinged with the sun,
And counted the moons as they rose and set
  O'er the ocean, one by one;
And they said to the winds, "blow ye swift and fast,
  And bear us nearer home."

But amid the bars of the music,
  That chimed with the dancers' feet,
A sound as of waves from their caverns loosed
  On the creaking timbers beat;

And the stern-browed captain staggered
   With a face that was ghastly and white,—
"We are fast on the rocks," he hoarsely said,
   "There is death on the sea to-night!
With never a gleam of moon or star,
   And never a beacon light!"

There was dread, and darkness, and terror
   On that grand old ship of the line,
With the breakers a-shrieking and roaring,
   In their fury all the time;
And pallid fathers striving
   'Mid the wild waves' anarchy,
On rigging or spar some darling to bear
   From old ocean's treachery;
And mothers seeking their babes that slept
   In their berths down under the sea.

In vain upon the taffrail
   The brave old captain stood,
Challenging there with his dauntless brow
   The demons of the flood,—
Calling his mariners, one by one,
   But they answered him never a word;
Never a word spoke the man at the helm,
   Or the sentinel on his guard!
Only the wind wailed fierce and fast
   Across the mizzen-yard.

The brazen bell through the watches '
    Of the long night tolled and tolled,
And the heavy guns to the pitiless sky
    Their fearful story rolled;
But never a message of mercy
    From the misty headlands crept,
To that doomed two hundred who struggled there
    Where the floods their orgies kept—
Where they sank in their deep sea sepulchers,
    In the solemn ocean crypt.
        O, the sea! the treacherous sea!
Man spreadeth the sails and stretcheth the shrouds
        Of his royal argosy;
But the mighty God, he keepeth the keys
        Of the citadels under the sea!

THE ARCTIC MARINERS.

*Sir John Franklin and two ships' crews left England
for the Arctic land in 1845, and never returned.*

The morn broke bright and brilliantly
    As that broad blue flag was spread,
And the last cheer sounded o'er the sea,
    And the last farewell was said.

A stern and stormy task was theirs—
Where the icebergs claimed their sway;
Where strange birds screamed the seaman's dirge
Through the long, long polar day.

But a wreath of fame was wove for them
When their perilous task was done;
And lightly they stretched the broad blue flag,
And gayly they journeyed on.

And lightly they vowed to return again
To the island amid the waves,
And to rest when their hardy toils were o'er
In their fathers' ancient graves.

But those dauntless words that the breezes bore
To hearts on the listening strand,
Were the last that greeted their native shore
From that doomed and that daring band.

They say that the red sun, mockingly,
Still shines in the shivering sky;
That the pale stars beam with a fitful beam
O'er the ice-reefs proud and high.

But neither the sun on the leafless plain,
Nor the stars on the frozen deep,

Nor the ice-crags piled o'er that Arctic main
Have told where the wanderers sleep.

And there's many an autumn's leaves turned brown
On their fathers' ancient graves;
But that broad blue flag ne'er shall stream again`
O'er that island amid the waves!

1850.

THE WATCHER OF THE ICEBERGS.

On the death of Lady Franklin, 1875.

Toll dirges from the minster bells—
Light torches in the chancel dim!
Let old cathedral organs burst
Into a grand funereal hymn!
And to that grand funereal hymn
The world shall send her sad refrain,
In hallowed gush of sympathy
Across the mountain and the main,
Where two proud oceans toss and foam,
Where plantains wave or snow-peaks loom.
Fair watcher of the icebergs lone—
For thee shall fall the tender tear,
Sweet lady of the silver hair!

We mind us of a day gone by
   When early youth was on our cheek:
On thine the kiss of him who turned
   The highways of the North to seek!
And all the flags in harbor furled,
   And all the loud guns, bade God speed,
Alas! unto the waiting world
   On every cliff-top taking heed;
Pausing of every wind that blew
   To question and to intercede.
No signal crossed the sea-mew's track,
   No voice from those dim solitudes,
   Where walrus herds or great auk broods,
   Across the rent floes drifted back.

And so through all the lengthening years
   Only to thy strained ear there crept
The shivering of the frosted shrouds—
   The quaking timbers torn and reft.
The signal-gun fired suddenly
   Far out across that silent sea;
The wasted mariner, whose voice
Woke neither echo nor replies,
   The frantic prayer tossed pleadingly
Across the dark sepulchral deep,
Whose dungeon doors their prisoners keep.

What marvel that the tress of gold
   Blanched through those withering years to snow?
That down athwart the midnight watch,
   The hand whose touch had thrilled thee so
Should beckon to thee through the haze
Of that impenetrable space,
   That trackless waste of frozen sea,
   Whence he might never come to thee.

And so with reverent heads we stand
   Within the vaulted minster's gloom,
And listen while the organ rolls
   Its dirges to the fretted dome;
Knowing that hand is clasping hand
   Somewhere amid the boundless spheres,—
That free, disfranchised souls have leaped
   The frozen barriers of the years,
And thus, 'mid orison and prayer
   Our souls sing songs of praise for thee,
Sweet lady of the silver hair!

INAUGURATED.*

Bonfires ablaze on the hill-tops,
  Banners afloat on the towers,
Flags sweeping high from the mastheads
  That guard these proud waters of ours.

Bells clanging loud from the steeples,
  Cannons a-boom from the height,
Wakening the echoing mountains,
  With tasseling forests bedight.

Son of the people, walk bravely,
  Up through the discord and din—
Up through the warring of factions,
  That shake our far borders again.

Up through the dust of the highways,
  Up through the darkling of storms;
Up through the crashing of tempests,
  Filling the land with alarms.

Bravely,—though here 'mong the marbles
  Crowding this Appian way,

* Hayes, 1877.

Martyrs have trodden the causeway
Thou hast been treading to-day.

Bravely,—walk bravely and grandly,
　Guardsman, whose watch must be kept
Lone on the ramparts of nations,
　By cyclones and hurricanes swept.

Wrap thy storm-mantle about thee,
　Stand with thy breast to the blast:
Let thy footsteps be heard down the ages,
　On the pavements that skirted the past.

And if through the smoke of the contest
　Thy turbulent pathway should lie,
Then may cohorts of angels attend thee,
　And the Lord of the Battle stand by!

———

A MAN OF MARK.

A man of mark and of force, you say,
　Well skilled in the law's most subtle phases;
With an eye that could scan in its scrutiny
　The densest shadows of legal mazes.

Well versed in the myths of polity,
　With a keener insight of men and nations;

A quicker glance at the secret strings
That move the factions in place and station,

Than falls to the average of men
Skimming across the world's horizon;
And he used for the greed of his selfish soul
The quicker sense of his subtle vision.

Well schooled in all polished codes and creeds
That fashion reads in her liturgy,
And playing with hearts as with strings of beads,
By friar worn for a rosary.

A man of polish and grace of mien,
With courtly smile and with civic air;
But guileful and deep was his soul, I ween,
And his life was false as his words were fair.

And yet, he kneeled in his cushioned pew,
Where sunshine glinted through frescoed arches,
With face devout as the sun looked on
Through many and many weary marches.

And when the patriarch, pleading late,
Prayed for the poor ones crushed, and many,
His coin dropped heavily in the plate
With the widow's mite and the poor man's penny.

And no man asked if the tithe were wrung
  From orphans who sat with their dead unburied;
They only counted the scrip he flung
  In the silver salver the deacon carried.

He stood with the fathers of the land,
  And sat unchallenged in highest places;
And watched with a rapt, devoted soul,
  The changing tides of financial phases.

And a grateful country will carve his name
  In lasting columns of chiseled granite,
And miles of plumes and sables wave
  When he takes his march to the other planet.

1878.

———

ONLY A COMMON MAN.

Not deeply versed in the lore of schools,
  Nor read in the cumbrous terms of sages,
Nor yet a slave to the servile rules
  That have governed the cringing world for ages.

No pet of fashion, no serf of creeds;
  No changeling, fast with the wild winds veering—

He only wrought for the world's great needs,
  And spoke true words for the sad world, cheering.

Yet on his brow, as he came and went,
  Men saw the mark of nature's peerage;
And knew that it bore no lie or feint,
  Or stamped the sands with deceitful mirage.

He seemed to climb the slippery rounds
  That false men climb to a high position,
But claimed the cause of the poor oppressed,
  And earth's cast-aways as his only mission.

Too brave of heart to sit aside
  And see the mass with their great wrongs wrest-
    ling,
Too noble of soul to strive for place,
  With paltry men the ranks contesting.

His hands were brown with the great world's work,
  And his heart was full of the sad world's labor;
But he wore no title beside his name,
  And he claimed no empty badge or favor.

No marble stands on the hills for him,
  The ancient trees alone wave o'er him;
But the stainless fame of his noble deeds
  Has gone to the other shore before him.

                                        1878.

SWEET EDITH LEIGH.

"Past the flower of her youth," did you say ?
  Her life is a garden of bloom!
And along the dusty wayside
  She scatters a soft perfume.   .

You judge her but as you see her,
  With her pallid cheek and brow,
And you know not the grandeur and depth of soul
  That slumbers on below.   .

We were mates in the by-gone summers,
  Sweet Edith Leigh and I;
Together we roamed the forests,
  And gathered the shells by the sea.

And she, like a bird of the tropics,
  With the rich deep bloom on her cheek,
Wove garlands of leaves for her sunny hair,
  And strings of shells for her neck.

And talked in her quaint wild fashion,
  In words that seemed to fall
Like the lingering rhymes of unfinished songs,
  Or some ancient madrigal.

Thus ever, with feet unstaying,
Paced merrily on the years,
And we dreamed not that life had courses
That were drenched with rains of tears.

Till one day o'er my Edith's threshold
A darkening shadow fell,
And she roamed no more by the sea with me,
Or the forest on the hill.

No more by the shores of the surging sea
Wandered a wayward wight;
But a woman's soul loomed up in her face,
Born of the pangs of a night!

For a helpless mother and little ones
Clung to her stronger hand,
And her noble father slept in his shroud
Long leagues across the land.

Did she quail and shrink in the tempest—
Did she sway like a broken reed?
Did she shiver and pale as the thunder-cloud
Broke over her sunny head?

No, but a strange light deepened
The blue of her earnest eye,
10

And she gazed with a far-oft glance, unawed,
  Through the blank futurity.

And with calm, strong faith in her spirit,
  And a sweet trust undismayed,
She wandered the dusty highways
  Undaunted and undismayed.

Undaunted, though thorns and brambles
  Her tired feet tortured so,—
And the roses forgot to blossom
  In the paths where she must go.

Still she gathered the gleams of sunshine
  With a tender and trustful hand,
For the darlings who looked through their tear-drops,
  And could not understand

Why the light of their life must perish—
  Be dashed from their sky at noon;
Why the bells must ring their dirges
  When the robins were all in tune.

Sweet Edith Leigh—those questions
  Rose stormily to *her* brain,
But she hushed them down, and to her tasks
  Turned steadily again.

And when the fair young mother
Drooped pensively, day by day,
And the autumn's crimson garland
On her early coffin lay,—

She folded the wee brood nestlings'
With a sob she durst not heave,
And the youth of her life she left behind
Upon her mother's grave.

There were summers and winters after that,
Coming with blight and bloom,
When the snow-drifts piled around her door,
Or the forests were all in tune.

And sometimes, when worn with toiling
And chafed with life's hard extremes,
The melodies of the distant sea
Came to her in her dreams,—

Came to her with soothing murmurs,
From out the beautiful years—
And she folded her darlings closer
And sang to them through her tears.

There was one who afar had loved her
As one might love a saint,

With the strong and patient love of years;
　But he uttered no complaint—

Only watched her with constant fervor,
　As one at the outer gate;
But ever she said, "the work of my life
　Calls for me, and I must wait."

So through the springs and the autumns
　She waited,—no thought of self
Wore fretful lines on her beautiful brow;
　No pining after wealth

Made callous and cold the chambers
　Of the heart she held her own;
But she bore her soul with a regal grace,
　No chances could dethrone.

There were blossoms within her lattice,
　And blossoms within her heart—
And the darlings she had nurtured
　Had grown to be a part

Of her heart of love; and when science
　To them threw wide its doors,　　·
She was prouder than any queen that walked
　Upon her marble floors!

A woman lofty of heart and soul;
Of royal stock was she!
And she filled up the pauses of the years
With gentle ministry.

"Past the prime of her youth," did you say?
There's no noble in all the land
But might bow in his stars and his plumes to her,
And bend to her command!

1877.

THE OLD MINER'S TALE.

Sit you down on the sea-shore, comrade,
Down on this rock by the sea—
Where the cormorant flaps his feathers
And the gull floats lazily.

And I'll tell you the tale of my life, boys—
Of those long, hard days, that are gone;
The tale that has changed my locks to gray
Ere touched by the westering sun.

For six long years in the gulches
I had wrestled hard with fate,

And toiled 'mid the stern, unyielding quartz
  From early morn till late,

Till my brow grew brown and dusky,
  And my hands grew hard with toil,
And my heart grew heavy and lonely
  Thinking of *home* the while.

Thinking of home and the dear ones,
  So far, so far away;
Over the hills with their purple light,
  And over the restless sea.

And wondering whether the dear old heads,
  Grown white as the winter's rime,
Were bowed in their evening prayer for me
  At the solemn twilight time!

And whether my brown-eyed Agnes
  Sat still in the cottage door,
Humming and tuning her song toward the West,
  While the sunbeams fell on the floor.

Well! I toiled, as I said, through the seasons,
  With a sad heart all the time,
For fortune smiled on my comrades' path,
  But she never smiled on mine—

Till one long August afternoon,
  As I threw my pick aside,
A sunbeam showed me a vein of gold
  Hid deep in the mountain's side.

There was never a living footstep near
  Save the vultures in the cliff,
And I bowed my head to my father's God,
  Who had pitied my lonely grief.

And when the rustling corn was ripe
  And gathered into sheaves,
And the proud magnolia on the winds
  Wasted her rosy leaves,—

I wrote one day to the fairy cot
  Afar on the English shore,
Where my Agnes sat 'mid the clustering vines
  That hung from the cottage door.

I told her my life was lonely
  In the fabled hills of gold;
For what is wealth or pelf to a man
  If his heart grows frozen and old?

And I bade her, as she loved me,
  Speed over the blustering brine,

And I would stand ready upon the shore
　To welcome the ship o' the line,—

Stand ready to welcome my darling,
　Whose soft brown eyes should be
As a guardian star through the night and the storm,
　As the light of heaven to me.

A ponderous seal of scarlet　　　.
　The eager message bore;
There was wealth in its folds, unstinted,
　For the loved on the further shore.

And I bade the ocean billows,
　And the winds, as they rose and fell,
Bear it safely and speedily onward
　To the cottage beneath the hill.

The months flew rapidly after that—
　I was busy lining my nest;
The prettiest perch you could light on,
　With the mountains in the West—

And the broad green sea before it,
　With its stretches of rock and sand:
And there I watched for the sails that blew
　Across from the fatherland.

Well, one fair day in the spring-time,
　A land-bound trader brought
Dispatches from a ship o' the line,
　Just heading for our port—

And a letter with odor of roses
　Fell fluttering to my knee;
'Twas a message sent by my Agnes,
　Told sweet and tenderly,—

"Watch for me," she said, "on the cliff-tops!
　A week from yesternight
I shall stand near the prow to hail you
　As the vessel heaves in sight.

"Stand ready upon the shore, love,
　To fold me in your arms,
For your darling is home-sick and weary,
　Breasting the ocean storms."

　　*　　*　　*　　*　　*　　*

stood that night on the sea-cliffs,
　The fierce gales beat and tore:
And the hurricane clouds through the threatening sky
　Their fateful omens bore.

And afar in the distance struggling,
　Half hid in the seething brine,

The fierce wind driving her outward,
  Loomed up the old ship of the line!

We watched her with pale, worn faces,
  And none of us ventured a word;
Could she weather the gale and make the port
  With such a sea aboard?

When suddenly spoke my comrade,
  In a hoarse, sepulchral tone,—
"The ship's a-fire! you can see the flame
  From her smothering hatches blown!"

Great God! how I shook in my terror!
  How I stretched my feeble hands!
How I called to the maddening winds to veer
  And drive her in toward the land!

But ever onward, and onward,
  She drove like a spectral thing,
And the stifled flames that had slept in her hold
  In the whirlwind's breath took wing.

They clambered aloft to the rigging,
  They mounted the quivering shrouds—
They climbed astride the giant mast
  And jeered at the thunder-clouds!

We launched a staunch boat seaward
  Amid the battling surf,
But the billows clenched her in their teeth
  With a hold that was fierce and gruff.

And the sturdy oar of oak I held
  With a wild, despairing hold,
Was tossed like a feather from my hand
  'Neath the crashing waves as they rolled.

They dragged me fainting shoreward,
  Where the curlew made her moan,
And when my wasted breath came back
  That blazing ship was gone!

I stood all night on the cliff-top
  And wildly spread my arms,
But my darling never came back to me
  From out of the ocean storms!

                                    1876.

A DAY OF DAYS.

Some days are writ in thunder—some in peace;
Some leave their trail along the dim horizon
In cloven lightnings, and the mad winds shriek
Like shrouded demons from their nether prison.

And some are painted with the tender brush
That touched the skies of Eden, azure tinted,
As where the clouds their carmine banners toss
O'er Alpine valleys, where the sunsets fainted.

'Tis such a day of days my soul recalls,
And on its witching splendor loves to ponder;
A day that lights with stolen glory all
The rugged passes of the highways yonder.

With skies that toned their ardent flashes down
With the soft mists of dim October hazes,
Flooding with purple tints the forests o'er,
Where the hushed birds sang whisperingly their
praises.

About my feet the painted leaves were heaped—
Amber and ruby, chrysolite and golden;

And both my eager hands the treasures heaped
  Like gold from eastern Bashaw's coffers olden.

I sat enthroned upon a jagged cliff,
  Full long ago deserted by the eagle;
Eaglets and eyrie their old perch had left,
  But near their roost, with wealth of banners regal

Floating above me, sat I through the hours
  Of that long peerless day in Indian summer;
Nor heard the strangled whispers of the wind
  O'er the deep seas, dread winter's wild forerunner.

Beyond me lay the lake—the dreamy lake;
  Cliff-sheltered Winnebago, where the spirits
Of her lone forest children walk and chafe,
  Amid the crags their sires did once inherit.

I sat expectantly, and soon beneath
 · And round me swept the ghosts of painted war-
    riors;
Each in his wampum-belt and heron's plume,
  Sought out their olden caves,—the ancient quarriers

Who delved amid those rocks 'neath the dim moons
  Of by-gone centuries, looked up and questioned
My right to hold the limestone precipice,
  Among the boulders of their rocky bastion.

I stretched to them my eager hands and said,—
"Now hold ye! Rest your bows and let us reason!
Give up the musty archives of your dead,
    And tarry ye, but for a little season!

"Tell me the mystery of yon battle-field, *
    Where dead men's bones lie tangled in the plough-
        share.
How many ages long has been their sleep?
    And wherefore met they in barbaric warfare?

"Which of you 'neath the elm-tree, by the lake,
    Lit up the council-fire with hemlock torches?
And called the ranks of feathered warriors back
    From the lone forest's ambuscade and marches?

"Why gathered not at midnight watch your hosts
    To wrest from alien Goths those lone mounds yon-
        der,
When the long silence of your heroes dead
    The iron-horse woke with its unearthly thunder?"

Long waited I upon my craggy perch
    For voice or answer—but there came no whisper;
Only the pheasant from her shy retreat,
    Conning so low her plaintive evening vesper.

---

* The ancient battle-field at the foot of the cliffs, on the
east shore of lake Winnebago.

The squirrel chippered from her nutting tree,
  Where her sage mate in monotones she chided,
And through the purple mists beneath my feet
  The airy hosts of painted sachems glided

In still battalions; while all alone
  I sat upon my throne of ferns and mosses,
Invoked the spirits of the ages gone,
  And watched the Winnebago where she tosses!

HALLELUJAHS ON THE HIMALAYAS.

"There shall be an handful on the top of the mountains
and the fruit thereof shall shake like Lebanon."

There was terror on the Ganges,
  And our palsied heart stood still,
For the demon-gods of Burmah
  Sat enthroned on every hill;
And the day was dim with horror,
  And the night was black with woe,
And each wind bore moans and curses
  O'er the sultry plains below.

We were but an handful scattered
  O'er that fateful land of doom,

And leagues and leagues of ocean
  Stretched on 'twixt us and home;
And we looked across the billow,
  But neither sail nor spar!
And the chariots of Jehovah
  We discerned not yet afar.

Then we gazed upon the mountains
  Frowning gloomily and grand,
Those ramparts of the ages
  Forged round that scorching land;
And we said, our great God reigneth
  Above the earthquake's shocks,
And he builds up "his defences
  In munitions of the rocks."

So we hied us to the fastness
  Of those solemn heights serene,
And with great keys of the ages
  Our strong God locked us in;
And with massive time-worn boulders
  Our lonely portals barred,
And battalions of the angels
  He left to be our guard!

And through days and nights uncounted
  We trod the mountain heath,
With the snowy peaks above us

And the jungles stretched beneath—
Where the air is dank and heavy
  With a pestilential breath,
And the valley of the Gunga
  Is the vestibule of death.

And the raven came and fed us
  In that silent mountain-keep,
While the scimetar and tulwar
  Crashed round us in our sleep;
And we knew our brethren slumbered
  All along the Goomtee's waves,
And we amid the passes
  Stood to guard each other's graves!

Still we looked into the faces
  Of the mothers, white with fear,
And we said, "our Lord Jehovah
  Is a mighty man of war;"
And we listened on the night-wind,
  And we listened on the breeze,
For the rustling of his banners
  Far across the foreign seas.

And when the boom of cannon
  Came thundering up the coast,
And through the teak and banyans
  Came the surging of the hosts—
11

And the Christians' flag unfolded
　O'er the minarets, all amaze;
Then we woke the Himalayas
　With a solemn song of praise.

And those hallelujahs echoed
　Ever since from hill to hill,
And o'er demon-haunted India
　Are grandly surging still;
And the handful on the mountains
　Has spread across the plain,
And our Christ shall rule the Orient
　From the mountains to the main.

[A small remnant of missionaries escaped to Nynee Tal
upon the Himalayas during the fearful Sepoy massacre in
1857.]

———

AT HALF-MAST.

The old bell shakes the Minster tower,
　The harbor flags at half-mast stand—
The grenadiers march two and four,
　With sable steeds caparisoned;
Toll forth, O bells! the message sent
　Throughout your creaking battlements,

For a prince within the chancel dim *
Lies waiting,—bear the exile in!

He may not sleep beneath the aisles
  Where his ambitious sires have trod,—
The land that watched his schemes and toils
  Spurns him from off his native sod;
The outcast's brand is on his brow,
  Hollow his grave and lay him low;
Let alien bells their dirges ring
  Where a son of France lies slumbering.

Came there no whisper to the ear?
  No echo of the distant sea,
Whose rocky isle alone—afar,
  Wakes up the ghosts of memory?
Proud race, of thought and purpose high—
  By nature formed to do and dare,
With plans all unachieved, that lie
  Smothered upon your early bier.

After the clangor and the storm,
  After the breakers and the surge,
Ye slumber well, where war's alarms
  Shall haunt ye never on the verge
Of that unfathomable life,
  Where prince and peasant meet alike!

* Napoleon III., buried at Chiselhurst, England.

IN THE WILDERNESS.

David Livingstone died in the heart of Africa, four-
teen hundred miles from the coast. His faithful
black servant guarded his body till it was safely
placed in Westminster Abbey.

Build me a hut 'mong the tangled brake,
  'Neath the lonely pampa's shade;
For my foot grows tired, and my heart grows faint,
  And the dark is overhead!

For long, long nights I have lain and watched
  For a breeze from the distant sea,
But only the breath of the wilderness
  Is borne again to me.

And when in my feverish dreams I hear
  The coast-bells ringing fast,
I wake, and 'tis only the ostrich's scream
  Through the desert flitting past.

And the same wild wish is in my heart,
  And the same faint, helpless cry—
"Let me see the cliffs of my childhood's home,
  And its green graves, ere I die!"

But the night came quick, and the night grew long
  In that weird and sultry wild,
And the eye of the chief was closing fast,
  Like the eye of a weary child.

And with many and many a league to pass
  'Twixt him and the surging sea,
They folded the sun-browned hands, at last,
  Of our hero, silently!

      *   *   *

    Toll, Minster bells!
  From your turrets, grey and deep;
For a prince of the world has passed away—
    Let him sleep!

    Let him sleep 'mong the lords of story,
  'Neath the heavy arches' gloom;
Through the palms and the towering banyans,
    They bear him home.

    Room for him 'mong the marbles
  Of your cloisters, dim and grand;
But his pillar is reared where the tamarinds rise,
    In that lonely land!

                      1876.

MICHAEL ANGELO'S LAST WORK.

With whitened brow, o'er which the snow had tram-
    pled
For four score years and ten, the artist sat,
And the dim halo of his incarnations
    About his lonely studio lingered yet.

Beyond him, where the yellow-crested Tiber
    Stretched through the land in deviating line,
Stood the proud dome his lofty thought had molded,
    Set high upon the battlements of time. *

And the world waited with a restless fervor
    For one more prophecy of art enshrined—
For one more legacy to leave the ages,
    Upon the speaking canvas boldly lined.

Men said, "the work-days of the seer are over,
    The unanswering canvass seeks his touch in vain;
And the great dream for which we long have waited
    Sleeps on unwrought within his misty brain."

But o'er the heavy arch that spanned his cloister,
    Across the frescoed roof a vision flashed;

* St. Peter's.

And the dim eye grew deep with inspiration,
   And the wan fingers o'er the canvass dashed

The lights and shades in wondrous combinations,
   Touched with the azure of the sunset's glow;
And waiting Rome said in her admiration,
   "The angels guide the old man's pencil now."

Along the Appian way, 'mid tombs of princes,
   His carved sarcophagus long ready stood in state;
Yet still he sat and wrought beside his easel—
   "The days are short," he said, "the grave must
     wait."

And so among the mists of evening gathering
   Deeper and deeper o'er his threshold store,
The old man plied his work among the shadows,
   Far through the midnight watches, all alone.

No weak decrepitude of soul, that clouded
   His last grand days with sad obscureness o'er;
He only laid his pencil down at evening
   To take it up upon the further shore.

                          1877.

THE OLD-TIME MINSTRELS.

We hear their songs go sweeping through the land,
  From fisher's cot to prince's marbled pile;
And the old minsters ring them soft and low
  From mossy towers, through dimly frescoed aisle.

But whither went the singers? Where away
  Died out the matchless voice that thrilled us so?
Ask the old hills, that on their summits grey
  Catch the red sunsets as they come and go!

Where are the harps that through the olden days
  Caught gladsomely your inspirations up,
And tossed them to the strugglers on life's highways,
  With gleams of beauty and with words of hope?

Earth's sagamen and soothsayers, whose thought
  Roamed the tall cliffs where the proud eagle built,
The echo of whose runes the listening years
  Along their musty corridors have felt,—

Can souls so glorious fade like myths away?
  Their dreams unfinished and their words half said?
And all the heritage they leave to us
  The mold and mosses on their coffin-lid?

Perchance if but our keener sense might catch
    The floating sound-waves, which the spheres beset,
Somewhere amid the upper ether stranded,
    Their thrilling melodies are ringing yet.

1878.

SLEEPING.

One of these crimson autumn days
    We shall be sleeping among the hills,
Where the midnight wind on its harp-strings plays,
    And the lonely wood-bird's echo thrills.
Sad eyes above us may watch and weep,
    Grieved hearts all round us may pant and swell,
Restlessly o'er us earth's tumults may sweep,
    But we shall have rest, and be still—be still,—

Under the shade of the solemn pine,
    Where the pale violets in spring-time are, ι
When the hazels are brown in the nutting time,
    And the tall vines clamber—it matters not where!
It matters not where, so the weary brow
    Shall throb and flutter, and flush no more,
So the spirit that chafes and tosses so
    Shall be hushed and calmed, and its moans be o'er.

We'll bid the wild weeds tangle and creep,
  And the snows lie thickly the long winter through;
And even the tempest to rattle and sweep,
  So they bring but a hush to the sleepers below.
And thickly,— blow thickly the red autumn leaves
  Above the blue violets and under the pines,
Wherever the cradle our earth-mother gives
    To her tired children sleeping the long twilight
    time!

THE WITCHES ARE WALKING THE WILD-WOODS AGAIN.

The witches are walking the wild-wood again,
  Down deep in the forest of pines,
Where the great goblin oak-tree stands lord of the
    glen
And where the winds sigh to the vines.

Old winter wrapped round him his mantle of snow
  And marched with his vanguard at last,
And the jay-bird peeped out through the tamarack
    bough
And screamed his farewell as he passed.

And quick from their coverts, the wild winds know
    where—
In highland, or hollow, or hill,
The weird forest witches came wandering there
    In the old woods, so solemn and still.

They peeped in the stream that had muttered and
    moaned
    As though summer was never to be,
And the light, laughing waves started off with a
    bound,
    And chased merrily on to the sea.

The brown tassels came to the larch-boughs again
    And the fur to the hickory buds,
And the poplar smiled forth in a garland of green,
    For the witches were walking the woods.

The oriole down in the clusters of cane
    Bethought him again of his nest,
And the whip-poor-will sang 'mong the hazels again
    When the sun had gone down in the west.

And dark brows, that all the long winter had kept
    Their shadows of sadness and care,
Laughed out to the glad summer sunshine that swept
    When the witches were wandering there.
                1856.

SUNDERED.

We have been friends! we have been friends
All through the wintry weather;
When skies looked black, and tempests came,
Still we were friends together.

But now the grasses seed and bloom
In the trysting-place of yore,
And ye might know by the wild-bird's tune
That we are friends no more.

1854.

BENEATH THE ELMS.

O, golden haze of the summer days,
That glints with glory my pathway over,
And forests that murmur like distant seas,
And clover-fields, peopled with honey-bees—
With patches of sunshine and moonshine flung
At sundown the silver waves among.

Why waketh no murmur within my soul
To the gladsome echoes that break and roll

Through the haughty oaks and the cloistered pine,
Where sleepeth the beautiful rhythm and rhyme
That my spirit caught in the olden time?

When a hymn was said, and a psalm was sung
By every voice as it swept along,
From the tempest that came with its shrieks and
     moans
To the brooklet that muttered among the stones;
And a solemn utterance seemed to thrill
The chords of my wakened soul at will.

I sit where the olden beeches meet,
And their golden leaves are about my feet;
I sit and wait for the old-time song
To murmur these autumn aisles along;
But only the jay-bird in the wood
Pipes up his lonely interlude!

Spirit of song! I conjure thee back!
To thy ancient nooks—to thy olden track;
For my soul is weary, and fretted, and sore,
With the surf-beats chafing upon life's shore—
With the storm-notes chorusing surly and dim,
Their sullen base to my beautiful hymn.

DOWN WHERE THE WATER LILIES GROW.

Mind you the place where the water-lilies grow, love,
Mind you the place where the water-lilies grow?
Where the willows hang their tassels, and the feath-
ery fern-leaves blow, love,
And the light wing of the blue-fly is skimming to
and fro?

'Twas there that I repeated the often-whispered story,
The often-whispered story that the ages love to
hear;
And the alders bent to listen, and the oak-trees grey
and hoary,
And the oriole and the robin, from their nesting-
places near.

And you promised in the autumn, when the sunset
tinged the beeches,
To sit within my cottage door and sing me olden
songs;
And I waited for you, darling, all through the wintry
weather,
And I wondered why the morning and the midnight were so long.

Sere grew the leaves, and a shadow came between
  us—
A lonesome shadow, resting around our trysting-
  tree;
And though the yellow glory has fallen on the
  beeches,
  Yet the oceans and the mountains have sundered
    you and me.

WHEN THE SUMMER COMES AGAIN.

When the summer comes again,
  There will be green graves and lonely,—
Little mounds upon the hill,
  Guarded by the hazels only!
Weedy sods, all hallowed made,
Where the last year's red leaves strayed.

When the summer comes again,
  There will be old trysts forgotten;
Vows that have been pledged in vain,
  Fondly spoke, but lightly broken;
Hearts that once beat warm together
Frozen in the summer weather!

When the summer comes again,
    There will be bright visions shaded—
Hopes that beacon-lights have been
    From the ocean reefers faded;
Stars, that wore a glory round them,
Paler now than when we found them!

When the summer comes again,
    There will be old haunts forsaken—
Cherished nooks in grove and glen,
    Whence the spells have all been taken,
Save when dreamy memories wander
'Mong the oaks and poplars yonder!

MY HOUSEHOLD CHOIR.

Sing to me, birds of mine,
From out your perches 'neath the household tree;
Sing to me snatches of some joyous rhyme,
Some grand old burst of solemn harmony.

Sing to me! let your voices
Keep rhythm with the waves that roll below,
While every forest chorister that warbles
Sends echoes from the oak-trees as they blow.

Sing to me some old psalm—
Some household ballad, or familiar hymn,
 Whose inspirations shall my spirit calm
From its wild turbulence—and soothe again.

For I am tired to-day—
Tired and o'erwearied with the toils of life;
 Counting its losses and defeats, and only
Longing too eagerly to quit the strife.

Sing to me, birds of mine,
Sing me glad songs, in voices sweet and cheery,
 Of "Eden shores," or "glorious Morning-land;"
Of "Rest, sweet rest," awaiting all the weary.

Sing me how "homeward-bound
The steady Pilot standeth at the wheel;"
 How 'mong our doubts, and fears, and griefs,
The pitying Father "doeth all things well."

How in the "land of rest,"
Upon the sands that skirt the great forever,
 There we shall meet "the loved ones gone before
 us,"
When safely o'er, we "Gather at the River."

1876.

THAT COTTAGE 'MONG THE CEDARS.

A low-roofed cottage, hidden most
   'Neath broad-leaved vines, that twist and tangle,
Where April swallows 'neath the eaves
   In mystic foreign accents wrangle;
Where to their quaint nests hid about
   Strays many a last year's brown-winged builder,—
And bees flit cheery in and out
   'Mid straggling branches that bewilder.
And that small cot almost forgot
   'Mong cedar boughs and clambering roses,
Sweet music murmurs round the spot
   At evening time when daylight closes.

And when the winds in petulance
   Sweep through the old trees, blossom-laden,
A perfumed snow-storm flecks the grass,
   Sweet as from spicy groves of Eden.
The purple grapes in autumn-time ·
   Hang down in many a heavy cluster,
And to the feast the golden-breast,
   And lark, and oriole gaily muster.
And that sweet spot, almost forgot
   'Mid cedar boughs and clambering roses,

Sweet music murmurs round the spot,
  At evening-time, when daylight closes.

And there, in summer's golden prime,
  When fresh sweet grasses lay in wind-rows,
A sunny nestling bird of mine
  Took perch within those vine-wreathed windows,
And twined white blossoms in her hair,
  And sang sweet songs in gentle measures;
And quaintly decked her sylvan nest
  With rustic art and wildwood treasures.
And that sweet spot almost forgot
  'Mid cedar-boughs and clambering roses,—
May storms sweep never o'er the spot
  Where sings my bird as evening closes.

                                        1878.

HARPS OF HOME.

Tune me the harps of home, minstrels of mine;
  Send some grand chorus o'er the mute strings
    sweeping!
Some glorious anthem, or some tender rhyme,
  In thrills along my slumbering pulses leaping,
    With all the ecstasy of olden time,
      Tune me the harps of home, minstrels of mine!

Tune me the harps of home, here in the watch
  Of the still twilight, with the moonlight falling,
Halting awhile amid the rugged march,
  Life's bugle-notes far in the distance calling;
    Strike up, my bards, some ancient battle hymn
    Before the morning wakes to fight again.

Some echo that shall linger sweet and long,
  A fresh impetus to my tired heart bringing,
Like the free cadence of a mountain song,
  That some glad bird upon the air is flinging,
    Tossing aloft the echoes that must roll
    In jubilant peans on from soul to soul!

1874.

WILL THE SUNSHINE COME?

Will the sunshine come when the storms are gone,
  And the spirit wakes up from sorrow?
Will the heart grow light when the dark to-night
  Is forgot in the bright to-morrow?

I know that the wing of the prisoned bird
  Can bound from the cage as free   .
As though it had roamed where the forests stirred
  Their leaves by the heaving sea.

But can the heart that has worn the chain
  So heavily and so long,
Tune its sad harp to wake again
  In a glad and joyous song?

Will the sunshine come when the storms are gone,
  And the spirit wakes up from sorrow?
Will the heart grow light when the dark to-night
  Is forgot in the bright to-morrow?

                                        1858.

TRAVEL-WORN.

And thus the days troop on—my days of leisure,
  Whose sunrise mocked me with its fairy haze,
With golden halos beaming o'er the heather—
  With peans of song and periods of praise.

With promised pauses in the weary marches,
  With gusts of inspiration from afar;
With soothing hushes 'mid life's busy clamor,
  Borne in amid its strange discordant jar.

But all fruitionless, with hurrying footsteps
  Flit the tired years, like spectral fleets away,

With jeering shadows mocking o'er the mountains
Of summer isles, and restful calms where lay

My fair ideal, locked in groves sequestered—
Shut in from all the hurry and the strife;
From all the turmoil and the petulant worries
Of this uneasy scene that we call life.

Oh, for a moon of calm and hushful quiet,
Where the o'erwearied soul fresh wing might take;
Where the hot pulses might forget their fever
Listening to ripples from the waves that break

Upon the cooling coastland, with the breezes
That sweep from labyrinths of pine and fir;
Where the grand canticles of ancient ocean
Might rise in mighty swells, above the jar

Of all life's shattered strings, drowning the clatter
That chafes our souls and wears the fretted chords;
And strangles in their birth the inspirations
That thought might clothe in grand, heroic words.

1878.